S

Of a Town

SMALL TALES OF A TOWN

SUSAN WEBSTER

*Collins
Publishers
Australia*

COLLINS PUBLISHERS AUSTRALIA
First published in Great Britain in 1988 by Simon & Schuster Ltd
This edition published in 1989 by William Collins Pty Ltd,
55 Clarence Street, Sydney NSW 2000

Copyright © Susan Webster 1988

National Library of Australia
Cataloguing-in-Publication data:

Webster, Susan,
Small tales of a town,
ISBN 0 7322 2492 6.
I. Title.
823'.914

All rights reserved. No part of this publication may be reproduced,
stored in a retrieval system, or transmitted, in any form, or
by any means, electronic, mechanical, photocopying, recording or
otherwise, without the prior permission of the publishers.

This book is sold subject to the condition that it shall not,
by way of trade or otherwise, be lent, resold, hired out or
otherwise circulated without the publisher's prior consent
in a form of binding or cover other than that in which it is
published and without a similar condition
including this condition being imposed on the subsequent purchaser.

Typeset in 11/13pt Ehrhardt
Printed by The Book Printer, Victoria

Contents

New to the Side	page	1
The Home Front		7
Molloy's Family Hotel		13
Rumour and Reputation		18
Boy on a Chain		24
Tam		34
Jack Mollison		39
Day of the Carrot		42
The Call to Freedom		46
Budgie Calls		54
Father and Son		59
A Fist of Fives		67
A Likely Contender		72
Power to the People		77
A Family Wedding		85
Now You See Him		91
Lot 57		100
The Voice of the Turtle		109
Lost Sheep		115
He Who Would Valiant Be		124
Loser Takes All		133
Bloody Waste		142
A Case for Dr Forbes		152
Sin City		162
Fanning Flames		173

New to the Side

Some people came here on purpose, but for most it was by chance. It was a town born of the wheatfield far about and flat; clinging low to the soil and lonely. From a distance it could not be seen from the surrounding plain for all the dust and shimmer kicked up by the summer heat.

It took an age to get there. The roads strung endless and straight in big open grids. Anywhere was a long way from anywhere else. And seventy miles from anywhere and edging up to the desert, the town hung on to the fringe of usable land as the last outpost before the big red dunes of the desert took command and nothing existed any more.

The red country was vast and shifting. The inching dunes would eat roads, slide over fences. Water-tanks would disappear. Animal bones long covered would emerge bleached stone-white and bitten through by the endless windblast of sand. And on bad days, when there was a westerly wind about, the sand would flurry into town like an angry red swarm and a wise man would lock up his house and take to the pub. There were many wise men in this town.

Molloy's Family Hotel and Beer Garden stood the tallest building, visible on a good day for many miles distant. It was a parody of a pub, wreathed in finicky lacework standing apart from the raw-hewn face of its red stone walls. It rose out of the plains like a signpost to misbegotten civic pride and had been a welcome vision for generations of travellers who found themselves in such an unwelcoming place.

Molloy's presided over Federation Street, a road stretching seven blocks to the north and south before surrendering out to gravel again. Two palm-trees marked the street's beginning and end, with a dry and bitter lawn between them. On either side the street was wide and empty, leading slowly past the garage, the Free Library, the chemist's, the newsagency, the police station and – down the other side of the street – Molloy's, the baker's, the food and farm goods store, the hardware, the butcher's and the Kookaburra Café closed, it seemed, for all time.

Midway along the street was the office of the *Weekly Advertiser*, a building barely the width of two armspans and facing out with sightless eyes of frosted glass. All the other buildings hid coyly and coolly from the sun under wide verandahs, but the words 'Weekly Advertiser' sat unprotected and sun-bleached against the stark, white-painted stone.

Hunting for a door, I found it down an alley to the side of the building. It was locked. By cupping my hand against the glass I could see inside along a narrow passage to a pigeonhole counter and walls painted pale grey, carrying a collection of yellowed posters advertising social football matches, bingo nights and Red Cross benefits. They were of universal design and all used the same typeface. One that I could read dated back three years.

Pasted up against the glass of the door were last week's photographs with the sign 'Order your favourite photos here.' A pork-barrel of a woman plumped full of country cooking was handing another a crocheted rug. Both beamed expansively at the camera. A boy, all angular limbs and kneecaps, squinted sideways into the sun as he held out a sporting trophy. There was a team-shot of some boys in football gear; a head-shot of a man looking uncomfortably tight in an unaccustomed suitcoat; and another, bulbous man in faded and tattered shorts holding a fish aloft. A kid in the background had pulled a silly face at the wrong time.

There was no chance of guessing the time and I had been several years now without a watch. I walked back to my car, switched on the radio and lit a cigarette, wondering all the while if this fellow Hegarty had forgotten about the interview.

Sunday afternoon was God Spot on the local radio station. An American evangelist rattled on, leaving barely a space for an intake of breath. I turned the dial.

' . . . And Lot 67 is a laminex table and four chairs, grey in colour and the condition is fair. Price is only fifteen dollars all up. That's fifteen dollars for this dining-room table and chairs. Four chairs that is. So, ladies, if you're looking for a new set of table and chairs for the kitchen, these are grey in colour and in a fair condition and fifteen dollars will get you the lot. If you want them you should phone a Nooweep number, the number is . . .'

All the wise men in town would now be sleeping off their Sunday roast, and radios across the country would be switched off.

I started to walk up the street, holding close to the windows and the shade of the verandahs. The windows of the Kookaburra Café were covered with white paper made waxy and brittle with time. The timber front bore darker patches where advertising signs had been. The window of the butcher's shop was bare save for some plastic sprigs of parsley and a toy cow. There was a sign saying 'Order your Christmas hams here' and a poster dissecting a sheep carcass into edible cuts. 'Printz & Sons – Butchers for Four Generations.'

There was a haphazard lean to the hardware shop that was accentuated by the jumble of goods pushing at the window from within. In the rear yard of iron fence and tumbled tree-trunks, long stretches of timber jutted outwards, scrap metal littered the yard and spilled on to the dirt path alongside. Sections of engines and parts of cars were recognisable, the rest was not. The shop windows were piled high with metal struts and angle-bent iron, rolls of weldmesh and wire and big paper sacks of nails still sold by the pound. One small corner had a display of kitchenware but it looked plastic and insignificant against the wave of more solid stuff. It was a shop of wooden floors, well worn.

Crossing the street, I stopped before the newsagency with its windows so crowded with slips of paper and hand-written announcements that it was barely possible to see inside. Notices for shower teas, benefit nights, bingo and hay-carting, baptisms, contract work and funerals – entire lives were strung out in the shop window.

'Won't do much good looking there.'

It was a man with faded blue eyes almost lost in a welter of creases. The face was so generally crumpled I had the immediate notion it had been forced through a washing mangle several times. There was a dewlap of skin hanging at each side of his neck and stretching slackly down to a set of very prominent collar-bones. It was as if all his skin had been roughly stretched and thrown loosely over his skull and skeleton. It was not at all attractive.

'The mongrel won't stock our papers so it's not much use looking in there for them. Good trip?'

Hegarty, Francis James. Printer and publisher and editor of the *Weekly Advertiser*, and, as his lapel badge boasted, Rotarian.

'Yes, thanks. Quite good. Long, but . . .'

'Four hours, five?'

'Longer.'

'Ah, after a while here you'll get to know the cross-country route. Longer in miles but a good twenty minutes shorter. Patches of gravel but fewer towns to slow you down. Not so many trucks. Might as well wander across.'

We walked back to the office under a sun that had drained the street of its colour, making it look flat like an over-exposed photograph.

'Why won't the newsagent stock the papers?' I asked.

'Just a snoot. Three years ago or thereabouts he got as cut as a cat and appeared in court. Then he turned up at the office saying if we printed the story he'd stop stocking the papers.' He turned the key in the lock, gave the door a belt with his fist and shouldered it open. 'So of course we ran with it. You go through, I'm just ducking to the toilet.'

Inside the thick stone walls it was cool and dark. Beyond the passage and the pigeon-holes was a frosted glass door opening out into a large room with blocked-in windows and a wooden plank floor that heaved at a slant. A couple of heavy black presses sat fat and slumbering in the darkened room. There was a slurry of ink and grime plastered over them and a chaos of fouled newsprint heaped underneath. A collection of old desks lay all scattered about with piles of paper, some kitchen chairs and, in one corner, a linotype machine looking as quaint and complex as one of those gaudy steam-driven hurdy-gurdy organs that featured in Victorian fun-fairs. It was a mastodon of black and silver, gleaming as the only clean piece of equipment in the room. I could not help but go over and stroke it.

'I told him to get out of my office and ever since we've been handling the newspaper sales from the front.' He came into the room doing himself up. His trousers, I noticed, had a button fly. 'And he's never talked to me since.' He was not a tall man, but in good proportion and with his clothes hanging off him a deal better than his flesh. Long and loose-limbed, he carried the same well-burnished suntan that everyone living up here came to possess. 'Pity. He was a good chap and a better cricketer. You play?'

'In a fashion.'

'We'd probably use you, then. Too many of us are getting too weak in the pins.'

'You mean you play?' I had guessed him to be no less than fifty years old.

'Give it a break.' He laughed. 'The side's not that hard up. I'm the incoming club secretary.' He pulled at a lever on the press, banging the side of the machine as he did so. 'Bloody apprentice. Thick as a side of beef. Good fielder though. Hands like flypaper. Follow me.' Pushing through another door, we entered a room so small and crowded I hung back at the entrance, unable to see a space to sit. 'I call it an office but I never was one much for words.' He laughed again. 'Used to be where we stored the accounts. Now Martha has them all stored in her head. Marvellous girl. Don't know what I'll do when she dies – and that won't be long either. You any good with accounts?'

I stuttered surprise.

'Ah well. I suppose when you apply to be a reporter you don't plan to balance the books as well. A man's only got one brain – and that's one too many in most cases. Are you going to take a seat or what?' He grabbed a pile of papers and dropped them to the floor, revealing a seat underneath. 'Don't mind the mess. I don't.

'Press day is of a Thursday,' he continued, 'except when the local races are on. They're mid-week races and we like to run final fields, so about four times a year we come out early on the Tuesday. We usually run sixteen to twenty pages and in October, when a chain takes over the Nooweep supermarket, there'll probably be an insert bumping that up to twenty, twenty-four pages.'

'That's the expansion you mentioned in your advertisement,' I said.

'Right.' He stopped a moment, looking at me askance and stroking the back of his hand against the desk. 'Look, I don't want to build it up too much. The job or the paper. This paper is old, it's well-established, but it's not *The Times* of London. I'm the editor by name but a printer by trade. I run the paper once a week to clean the presses. You run the paper once a week to fill the white spaces between the advertisements. You know the wage, you've seen the product. It won't win awards but it's read like the Bible hereabouts – and the Bible is read hereabouts. Don't shake them too much, and spell their names right. That's about all there is to it.' He spread his hands on the desk, staring at the veins and bones cast out in high relief from the slack skin. 'Still interested?'

Mortgage companies would take time to find me way out here. With a stay of execution and a salary advance I could dodge repossession. 'Yes, but don't you want to see more of my cuttings, references?'

'No. That stuff you sent with your application was good enough. Can you drink?'

'Can a lion cease its roar?'

For a moment a puzzled line divided his eyebrows and his mouth set blankly. Then his lips slid away from his teeth, and his teeth parted to emit another of his brittle, fractured laughs. 'You'll do fine, just fine.'

Suddenly he rose and made for the door. 'See you tomorrow then,' he said, pointing me the way out. 'You'll have to excuse me, need a piss. Bloody Japanese bladder.'

The Home Front

Being a man of wildly changeable moods, Hegarty proved himself a boss to be handled with flexibility.

'Flexible? I'd say. Like a fornicating ballet dancer,' said Pat, the bromide operator whose one-time wealthy upbringing and private schooling had bestowed a lively interest in crudity. When he spoke it was a conversation bridging the gap between Aristophanes and soft porn. I enjoyed talking with him a great deal.

It had been a torrid morning in the office of the *Weekly Advertiser*. An advertisement for the Red Cross had carried the wrong telephone number, I'd printed the wrong date for the next Rotary meeting, and a photograph of Mr Tilson – owner of Tilson's Reliable Garage – had turned out with a dag seemingly dripping from his prominent nose.

Hegarty, being a Red Cross patron, a Rotarian and a drinking mate of Tilson's, had no fair words for any of us that morning. He stalked into the room muttering something about 'pack of scums' and 'bunch of bloody girls' and disappeared into his office.

Pat ambled over with a racing form circled with the tips he was offering. The fields were looking tight but – with the unswerving attention he paid to such things – Pat had lifted a few horses out of the bunch for gentle consideration.

'Wouldn't consider them for more than a tenner though,' he said. 'The odds are tighter when the river's in full flood.'

In the first weeks of working here I had already learned this statement described the rectal elasticity of a fish going backwards up Niagara Falls.

'How long have you worked here, Pat?'

'Rising fifteen years,' he said, lapsing into racecourse jargon.

'Is it serious when he gets like that?' I asked, indicating the closed door to Hegarty's office.

'You won't need another fifteen years to know that answer. Leave it another hour.' And he was off back to his camera-room where there were several telephones on separate lines and the odds he offered were a sight more generous than anywhere else in town.

It took more than an hour. It was almost noon when Hegarty's voice called for me, and then he sounded so untroubled I could't believe it had been him storming through the office that morning.

'Have you found a place to live yet?'

I told him I hadn't, adding that Molloy's – while being a fine old institution in this town – was not always the quietest. And over the years it had yawned and sighed on its foundations, growing yet more gaps in the window seals, certainly more than it was humanly possible to plug at one time. Besides, it was accommodation offering a most awful temptation and the cause of more than one sore head the next morning as I prepared for work. That point, however, I didn't explain to Hegarty.

'I think I can help you then,' he said. 'Peter Spratt was talking to me last night and said there's a place over at Grigg's Corner. It used to be the family place but he doesn't think there's anyone in it now. Could be worth a look.' He rose from his desk and went to the large, detailed map pinned to the wall. I watched the bony knuckle of his right index finger trace the road out to the place and could not help thinking he must have suffered some peculiar bone disease at an early age.

'Of course, it's up to you, but I might say that it's a fair way out and if you need to come into town quickly you'll have to fly. Also, you're on the other side of the river. It's no worry in the dry, it drains down to the bed, but you could have troubles when the flash floods come through in the wet season. Anyway, I told him I'd pass on the news to you.'

I was far away, remembering my days in the suburbs when the only obstacle was a string of obstinate traffic lights and an occasional police speed-trap near the supermarket car park. The prospect of fording floods and tearaway races across forty miles of dirt roads seemed as distant as Mars. But I thanked him.

'Hang on a moment. I was thinking of this the other day, but

I might as well raise it now,' he said. 'You know there is a boarding house in the town. Well, not really a boarding house – not on her tax returns – but Mrs Evans, George Evans's widow, takes in lodgers to cover her costs. Huge, rambling place just beyond the meatworks. Might be worth a visit. Some of the railway gangers stay there when they're posted up here a while.'

I took down the information and left just as he picked up the ringing telephone. It might be another angry Rotarian.

The morning mail had been sorted and a few envelopes sat on my desk. Some had clear panes and I did not wish to read them, so I filed them in the bin. Some were sports reports: others were nattily-typed press releases from ever-hopeful advertising agencies with too much money and too little nous to realise that, when it came to column space, their wares had nothing on the might of the Nooweep Hospital charity committee report.

The last envelope I recognised for the fine, spidery handwriting of my mother. A woman of poor but proper education, she wrote in loopy, old-fashioned copperplate script and laid out her letters in a classically formal style. Reading them always evoked images of children huddled over wooden desks laboriously copying texts from script manuals and seeking perfection in the downward strokes of their fountain pens. It was only recently that my mother had switched to ball-point after years of nibs and ink-wells.

She opened by inquiring of my health and reminding me that a salt-water gargle was the best prevention for sore throats. My childhood had been one of general good health peppered, nevertheless, with spates of curatives administered in my mother's unshakeable belief that something was bound to go wrong sometimes. As a result I had been weaned on molasses, force-fed cod liver oil and once shamed at school with a crew-cut when my mother suspected a nits plague. Spurning modern medicines, she insisted we children flush our systems with eight glasses of water daily, clean our teeth with salt, and plaster any infected cut with a poultice of softened soap mixed with white sugar – a remedy, oddly, that worked excellently.

I had survived her care into adulthood and, after leaving home, continued to survive. Her letters, however, still carried suggestions as to how to ward off almost every disease except cholera – and only that, I suspect, because she had never thought it a disease of the white man. She was a remnant of another time.

The letter I held was praising the virtues of an extra blanket folded at the foot of the bed for chilly nights and the restorative powers of poached liver. I muttered a silent thanks that my mother had never discovered enemas. She continued on with news of the family: the ingrown toenail of an aunt had finally healed, an uncle was finding his wind coming much easier since he'd been inhaling peppermint tea. Charles, whose relationship I'd never fathomed beyond a second cousin once removed, was pulling out of a prostate operation. The vegetable garden had survived an invasion of dill that mother had planted two seasons ago in the belief that the seeds would cure flatulence. Apparently they did, but displayed a startling fecundity and had overtaken most of the plot by the following season.

She concluded by saying how pleased she was that I seemed happy with the job. She hoped that I would be settling down soon, approaching as I was an age where such things mattered. She asked if I had a telephone and then announced that she would be arriving next week for a visit.

It was a casual proclamation and a devilish sleight of hand. She slid it into the mass of the letter like a pill in a spoonful of jam. I was over a barrel. I had one week to get out of Molloy's and find a home – at least for the duration of her visit. I would have to see these places that afternoon.

Overblown Gothic would best describe the house. Built sometime Edwardian, I suppose, its various additions documented architectural change since that time. The buckled walls of red brick, wooden board and iron sheets cast up a variety of shadows along its rambling length. Windows blurred through years of grime stared blankly on to the street. The front fence twisted between dry thickets of dead hydrangea. An overgrown boxthorn cascaded over the side fence and threatened to topple it with its weight. Foot and wheel tracks cut through the long grass and there was a broken, faded wooden sign on the front gate. 'TRESPASSERS W', it warned.

The mesh of the fly-wire door curled away from the frame. I could hear the sound of a television coming from one of the rooms off the dark, central hallway.

Knocking several times brought no response. I knocked louder and called, 'Hello? Hello?' I heard a shuffle like loose slippers across a linoleum floor, a cough, and the television quietened. I knocked again. 'Hello? Hello? Mrs Evans?' I pulled back the door and stepped inside the house. It had a smell about it that suggested cats.

Further down the hall was a small table strewn over with papers and long-dead letters. The telephone was locked, and pinned to the wall was a notice: 'Your calls – your paying. Local calls only. Get key from me.'

A door was opened behind me by a vast downward dollop of white flesh forced tightly into a flowered cotton shift. From the top of her dress two arms swelled like two great thighs. Her face I hardly noticed, my attention catching and fixing on the thick growth of black hair on her upper lip.

'Mrs Evans . . . ?'

'Maybe,' said the woman. 'Who do you want?'

'Oh. I'm not sure,' I said. 'I want to ask Mrs Evans, or someone, about a room.'

'A room. Just a room?'

'Well, I was hoping for a room with a shower, or even a basin.'

There was a long silence. 'A room with a basin,' she said. 'And who do you want?'

I was starting to feel my voice tighten. 'I've told you, Mrs Evans.'

'And I've told you she's not here. Who else?'

'Who else should I see?'

She pushed open the door behind her, watching me all the while. Inside, a gaunt woman sat tightly folded into a chair. She was a blonde, but not a blonde from birth.

'Marie, and Pauline.' She pointed to another blonde drawing on a cigarette. 'And Stella.' She pointed to an Aboriginal girl— possibly half-caste—who sat behind the door drinking a cup of coffee. They did not speak and only looked at me.

'Which one of you should I speak to?'

'How much?' asked the large woman.

'How much are you wanting?'

'Twenty.'

'What about extras?'

She looked at me a moment. 'No, no extras here. Just twenty and that's all.'

'So it's everything for twenty a week, then?'

'A week?'

I was surprised. 'Not twenty a day, surely?'

The large woman looked suddenly churlish. She closed the door and planted herself in front of me. I suspect the width of her chest stopped her from crossing her arms.

'How did you come to come here?' she demanded.

'My boss told me that Mrs Evans takes in people.'

'Has he ever been here?'

'I don't know. I don't think so. His family have had their place for years.'

'But has he ever been here?'

'I don't know. He may have.' There are times I wish I was blessed with greater insight. There are times I wish I would listen to my instincts.

'Your boss – he works on the railways too?'

'No he doesn't.'

'Do you?'

'No.'

'Then why are you here?'

'I'm looking for Mrs Evans because I'm looking for somewhere to live . . . like the railway gangers who live here.'

'They don't live . . .' She stopped. 'You're here for a room and a basin and that's all?'

'Yes.' I think it was then that I realised.

'All the rooms are taken,' she said, sharply, and shepherded me to the door.

'I think I might try for somewhere else.' I reached for the door.

'Good idea.'

There was a man at the door. 'Afternoon, Mrs Evans. Pauline in?' And the force of something large pushed me out on to the street before I heard the reply.

Molloy's Family Hotel

Mick Molloy had the knack of a publican. He was doing you a mighty favour as he took away your money. The happy surrender of hard-earned pay – and the frequency of it – defied logic. Micky knew how to coax it out of trouser pockets.

When he served fry-up for Friday lunch he ensured that the town's Catholics remained customers. He simply absolved them. 'Fish, this stuff. Pure fish.' He ladled out the left-overs, mashed beyond recognition, fried and made fragrant with butter. The smell alone would set your gastric juices off in four-part harmony. 'Pure fish. Not a scrap of meat in any of it.' And the rest of his patrons would vouch for the fact, waving their forks noisily aloft as proof. If one Catholic was to burn in Hell for the transgression, so should we all.

Other men might die for their faith; here a man faced stiffer judgement. It would come not from that final parry with the cherubims and seraphims but from daily scrutiny by his fellows on earth. It was that knowledge, and that fear, that made real sins rare.

Pat was seated at the bar, his heels hooked over the foot rail and his concentration fixed upon the form book as he tried to estimate his chances with the weekend races. He was born with bookmaker's luck; his attendance in church each Sunday was merely a contributing factor. I watched him with idle attention, feeling tight-belted and contented. Around the bar sat men slowly digesting the newspapers. Others sat in undisturbed corners and closed their eyes to contemplate the greater feats and follies of mankind.

Even Pam, the barmaid, was excused her lassitude as she flicked at flies with a damp tea-towel. It was as much energy as she could exert at one time, and she didn't score many hits, either.

The insects flew in through the open door and windows and clustered in the centre of the room, hovering between the shafts of dark and light. The soft and continuous hum of their flight was the only breach in the silence, save the occasional sweep as a page of the newspaper turned. Far away a dog barked and a crow cawed at the sky. Within the closeted front bar the customers were deep in their private contemplations. This was not a place for lively times. For the most part the locals had to content themselves with the excitement of watching the figures ticking over in the petrol pump at Tilson's Reliable Garage. At this moment, however, even that was a dash too exciting for us.

Pam stopped her persecution of the flies and went to sit at the far end of the bar. One of her targets landed close to my elbow and, after a short inspection of the bar top, delicately set about its toilet, rubbing together its spindly hind legs. In the surrounding silence I could almost swear that I heard the sound of those abrasions. But I could not be sure. It was a fastidious and exacting job, and only when it was finished did the fly start cleaning its head. Again and again it bobbed as it wiped at the surface of those extraordinarily large and multi-faceted eyes. As the head turned, a complex pattern of colours reflected back from the countless lenses.

I drew my head almost indecently close to watch, gently resting my chin on the bar to support the weight of my head. I scarcely drew breath in case it should ripple past and disturb the creature, which was now cleaning its forelegs, holding them up in an attitude of prayer and then rubbing them together furiously, like a miser gloating over his hoard.

At first I did not recognise the sound of my name, nor the voice that called it. Pat had to jab my side with his finger before I broke off my concentration from the bar top. He indicated the door with a nod of his head. My mother called my name again.

'I'd get her out of here if I was you,' Pat murmured behind my ear.

With my belly filled and my senses dulled, I was too sluggish to move in time. She had already crossed the threshold. She commanded a good deal of attention as she walked into the room.

'Mother,' I said, unsure if the muscles of my face were pulled into a smile or a grimace. 'Mother, we must go...' I was projected from my seat and across the floor by a push from Pat. A couple of old farmers had woken with a start and one started to wheeze dangerously from the shock.

'We must go to the office,' I said.

'I'd dearly like something to drink,' she said. Her voice was clear and bright. 'I've been driving most of the day.'

I caught her arm and directed her again towards the door. 'Come, Mother. You shouldn't be here.'

'Why not?' called out one wag with an interest in my embarrassment.

'Yes. It's not against the law,' said another.

I gripped her shoulders with more determination. We were not going to be the afternoon's entertainment if I could help it.

'Actually,' she said, stopping me with a shy smile, 'I'd like to meet some of your friends.'

'These aren't my...'

'And we'd like to meet his mum,' said Sayers, smiling with unconvincing gallantry. 'What would you like to drink, missus?'

Mother giggled and demured until, like a child at Christmas, she said, 'What I would really like is...' and held her breath as she surveyed the shelves, '... a sweet sherry shandy.'

They bought her a double.

'Remember the days when a woman wasn't allowed in the main bar?' said Pat.

'My oath,' said young Sayers, 'that was a long time ago. In those days girls used to say "yes" to me.'

Mother looked at him. 'And what do they say now?'

'Yes please.' He gave a sly and whiskery laugh.

They bought her another round and, in the knockabout din, I whispered to her, 'I thought I'd be seeing you at home, Mother.'

She waved a dismissive hand. 'Oh, I couldn't follow your directions. It all looked like cuneiform – quite primitive.' She took another sip. 'This sherry is... memorable.'

'What do you mean – primitive?' I believe there was an edge of annoyance to my voice.

'Yes... I shan't forget this sherry in a hurry,' she continued, eyeing her glass dubiously. 'All those unmade roads.'

'One.'

'And rivers...'

'Barely ankle-deep.'

'Turning at this crossroad and watching for this silo – that shed...'

'They're really quite distinctive. You get used to it,' I said.

'I believe you are.'

'Are what?'

'Getting used to it. I always knew your heart wasn't in the city.'

'And his wallet's in bloody Vladivostok. Must be his turn for a round – isn't it?' said Pat, with a hint of vinegar to his smile.

'You're probably a bit like your father in that,' she continued, pushing her drained glass at me. She had the relentless drive of a tank – and the thirst. 'In fact, you know I'd almost forgotten it, but he was up this part of the world in his youth. Quite a while, as I remember it. He was a wild one then, and travelled with the teams of pickers and shearers. I quite literally picked him up one day from the middle of the road – dead drunk and flat broke. But my, he was so handsome. Quite a lad, that one.' She took a thoughtful swig as if to be toasting his memory. 'Stayed quite a while up here, actually. At a place called Tingalla.'

The bar went suddenly, absolutely still. She commanded a lot of attention – and not all of it friendly – when she invoked the name of this town's arch-rival.

The water was murky in Tingalla and the beer was flat. The pub was unfriendly and the petrol-station pumps were rigged. The saleyards, the schools, everything about the town was bad – according to the savants of Molloy's front bar. And Tingalla had a pinball machine in the café; an evil temptation for young people with better things to do with their time and money. Tingalla bred hoodlums and juvenile delinquents – and its adult population was no better.

'Did I say something wrong?' Mother looked around the hushed room and then continued, innocent of her crime – or the knowledge of it. 'I'm afraid he didn't stay there long, though. He... how do you say it? He left under a storm.'

'You mean under a cloud,' said Freedom.

'No... it was a storm,' she said. 'They had made him treasurer of the Tingalla Cricket Club and he... Oh, but it was a long time ago.'

'What did he do, missus?'

'They made him treasurer and then he left.' She concentrated on tucking back her hair, patting at it constantly. 'He borrowed some of the club funds and forgot to repay them. He was always a bit absent-minded like that. Killed him in the end. Forgot his heart tablets one day and just keeled over at the barber's. Gave the poor old barber such a turn.'

Pat drew the attention of the bar to himself by standing on a chair and proclaiming loudly, 'I feel that we should toast the good man's memory. Any man who commits so reprehensible a crime as stealing the funds of the Tingalla Cricket Club . . .'

'Shame!' came the cry.

' . . . should be saluted for his courage and his good taste, wouldn't you say?'

A cry of agreement went up.

'Furthermore,' he continued, 'I feel that the son should atone for the father's sin.'

Louder cries came from the front bar – all agreeing and raising their glasses at me. I felt an arm or two slip around my shoulders. It seemed I had been bonded.

If I was the hero of the moment, it was by proxy. It was also very expensive. Mother, seeing how the memory of the miscreant was lightening my wallet, tucked a few notes in my hand, whispering, 'I'd be careful when I walked the streets of Tingalla.' She straightened and smiled at the rest of the drinkers, murmuring aside to me, 'Say thank you to your mother.'

'Thank you, Mother,' I replied, dutifully.

Rumour and Reputation

The town was not a small one, but small enough when you'd done something wrong.

The network of news and gossip had manifold tentacles reaching beyond Federation Street to the farms and outlying settlements. But it flourished most healthily in the environs of the main street and most particularly in the front bar of Molloy's.

It had taken little time for the news of Ted and Peter Maguire to get around, and I suspect I heard it only after the story of the two men's fight had been discussed in ample detail over dinner tables around the district. I heard it from Morrie, who said he'd been told by his elder son, who doubtless would have picked it up from someone at the cricket club, and that virtually guaranteed that everyone around knew.

The Maguire brothers farmed together a stretch of more than 800 acres – mostly barley and some sheep. Their father had done so before them, and their grandfather too. Their farm was not a model one, operating more through the vagaries of inspired bouts of slog scattered through long periods of inactivity. They were always talking of selling and going into beef country up north. They talked of that a lot. Something they talked less of than was commonly supposed was their domestic situation.

Both were approaching their late forties. A lifetime on the land had etched such lines into their faces and so strung out their bodies that they appeared older. They were bachelors both, and touchy characters to boot. They regarded few people as friends and in that number did not really include each other.

Their speech to each other was always clipped and practical, more like that of work acquaintances than siblings.

Some years back the gossips had learned of the housekeeper they had taken in to bring order to the large family house they had inherited. She was a woman also of about forty years. Divorced or separated, the tongues of the town could not decide. But she was single and, living in the house with Pete and Ted, a subject ripe for speculation.

Talk of this woman remained an intermittent subject of public interest, despite the fact that she appeared not to hold much for pubs and women's clubs and kept pretty well out of the public eye. She was called Brenda, although the Maguire brothers had sometimes been known to refer to her as 'the woman', without any emotion or further explanation. It seemed she fed them well and kept them patched and washed when it came to clothes. No one much visited, but it was said she had worked like a Trojan to scrub the house clean of decades of muddy boot-prints and generally spruced up the place no end.

And so it continued until one Monday lunch-time, when Morrie leaned across from his regular roost at the front bar to tell me what his son had heard.

'You've heard about the Maguires then?' he said.

'No, what?'

'About the blue.'

'Haven't heard a thing.'

'Pete's in hospital and Ted's shot off. Gone to Sydney they reckon.'

'Why, what happened?'

Morrie told the story drily. Things like this happened too rarely in the town for dramatics to get in the way.

The previous Thursday Pete had gone to the sheep sales and was still away by the afternoon, when Ted came back home from levelling some paddocks. Brenda had told him she was quitting. It seemed some aunt in Melbourne was coming out of hospital and needed someone to stay with her. Ted had said fair enough and suggested a beer to mark the event. By late evening they'd sunk a few and were getting pretty close about things in general. Pete must have come back from the sales at this time and it seems that they didn't hear him come in, what with her talking about the shift and him not talking a great deal but saying a lot in other ways and what have you.

What happened then, Morrie wasn't too sure. It seemed that Pete got it in his head that the pair had long planned to make a break and that his brother was suggesting that this would be a good time for them to leave the farm – and Pete – in the lurch.

'Not having been around in the beginning to hear she was leaving anyway,' Morrie said. 'And probably not being able to understand if he had have heard. Blokes at the sale that day said he'd been in the bar most of the time.'

He said Pete had grabbed hold of a fence-strainer or something heavy like that and lurched on to the pair of them, swinging this thing around and bellowing like a stung bull all the while. Apparently he did a bit of damage to the kitchen and, in the thick of it, managed to do himself an injury in parts of the anatomy a bachelor farmer doesn't much use.

The woman shot off to Melbourne on the first morning train. Someone had seen Ted gunning up his pick-up, Sydney-bound. It was said that Pete had booked himself into the hospital some time that night, saying how he'd injured himself on the tractor. But in a bout of self-pity he had told old Mrs Warrington what really happened, and it was soon over town.

'It'd make you laugh,' said Morrie, turning back to his beer. I agreed. Later I wish I hadn't. It was my turn next.

I had been out to Wirralla for a job and was in no great hurry on the return trip, arriving back at the office a good four hours later. It had been a fine day, clear and sunny and not too hot, so I unleashed the car a bit and sailed over many flat miles listening to the radio and thinking of nothing much.

From under a cloudless sky, I came in to an office inexplicably dark. Martha's face appeared from her pigeon-hole like a Gorgon with a bout of dyspepsia. Her frown and stony silence followed me as I pushed through the door into the print-room. The men there stopped to watch me as I nodded and walked through to my office. They spoke no words and I figured it best to stay out of the light for the rest of the afternoon. Whatever was annoying them, I wanted no part of it – probably the failure of a favourite in the city races that afternoon and the sudden accumulation of wealth by Pat. I must ask what odds he'd been offering.

I waited for them to finish the day before hunting him out.

There was a red light on outside the camera-room to show that Pat was either working or taking a consideration from a customer. I knew which, and knocked. He seemed less than happy at the sight of me.

'Have you got time for a word?' I asked.

'Just wait there,' he said, returning to finish his phone-call. Then he beckoned me in. It was odd for a man with good reasons to keep his room out of bounds, but I entered. He closed the door, locked it, and turned off the main light. The vast bromide camera was humming in the corner. It was a small room, made hotter and closer by the machinery jammed into it. I perched on the table and felt under my right hand a bank of five or six phones necessary for Pat's other business.

He stood at the other side of the room and I could see the outline of his profile against the safe light. I was not feeling at all comfortable.

'So, what's up?' I asked.

Pat, for a rare moment, seemed to rein back his words. 'Your wife's solicitor called in today,' he started slowly. 'Reckons that if you don't shell out the alimony he's going to drag you to court.'

I gaped widely, unable to speak.

'Reckons you owe nearly twenty thousand dollars, for the five kids and her.'

My voice made grunts. 'Five . . . wife . . . kids?'

'If you don't mind me saying, and I'm going to say it anyway, it's a lousy trick and you deserve snotting. But that's all I'm going to say to you. You'd better get out now.' He went to open the door.

'I don't have a wife,' I gurgled. 'And no kids.' He turned to watch me. 'Pat, I'm single.'

He rocked back on his heels. 'Normally I'd wink and say "cunning devil". I'd more likely hand you a fist of fives, coming to this job saying you weren't married.'

'But I'm not, there's no wife and no kids. Never have been.'

'Well then, the wife you don't have phoned up here about noon to check that the lawyer bloke had been, and Martha said she heard a baby crying in the background.'

I couldn't answer.

Pat held the door open. 'I'd wait until dark before I got away. No use giving them something more to talk about. And I wouldn't walk through the front door of Molloy's. It'll be all over town like a drippy dick by now.'

'Pat, tell me again, slowly, what happened when I was out. Christ, I can't believe this. Look, mate, as honest as I can be, I have no wife and no kids. They've got the wrong person. They must have.'

Pat stood silent, but it almost seemed like he was warming. 'About eleven,' he began, 'this bloke came in and went to Martha and asked to speak to you. Asked for you by name. She told him you were out. He was a lawyer from Melbourne, blue suit, tie, fattish and some hair. Had a briefcase too. He asked when you'd be back and then told Martha you had to contact him urgently so he could list the case in time for the next Family Court sitting. Then he told her about the wife, the kids and the money.'

I listened, and began to understand.

'Well, us in here got to hear of it and – well, to be honest, if you'd walked in here that minute you would have had to have been taken away in an ambulance. They're big on families around here.'

'Go on.'

'Then, just after lunch-time, this woman phones up and Martha said she heard the long-distance dial tone. She asks her if this lawyer had showed up yet. Sounded real desperate, Martha said, and there was a tiddler howling in the background.'

I felt the air coming into my lungs again. 'And what about the car?'

'Well, one of the boys saw him stopped in the street and climbing out of a green Beetle, one of those clapped-out Volkswagens. I thought it a bit strange, lawyers getting more than a new bride and what have you.'

I started to laugh, light-headed with the aftermath of fear. 'Oh' – I was clutching at my flank where the stab of pain had doubled me over – 'the right bastards. I love them ... Pat, we have just seen two people – old friends of mine keen for a practical joke – deceive the whole staff of the newspaper. Steve is a fattish forty and drives a beat-up old VW as green as we are.'

Pat seemed almost capable of sharing the joke.

'And Carolyn, his wife, has just had another little bundle of joy. I'd take any odds you'd care to offer that she was my distraught wife phoning from Melbourne. They caught us all out.'

'If that be the case,' Pat began slowly, 'they've gone and tricked the whole town too. And that means they've destroyed any chance you have of getting a social life up here, mate. Unless you manage to get the explanation around the place and, more important, unless you can get everyone to believe it, you're out on a limb. And unless you can get all that to happen you won't be getting your end in anywhere within a sixty-mile radius of this town.'

The laughter died in me. This was serious.

'It'll only leave the sheep for you, my boy. And all the good ones are taken. You'll get an ugly one.'

We both laughed, and we kept on laughing, we could not stop. Only towards midnight did I stagger out of the camera-room, still laughing, after taking liberal doses of the reviving Irish malt Pat kept stored for occasions such as this.

Boy on a Chain

With all the backhand irony endemic to a town like this, the newspaper photographer was known as 'Zoom'. He had once been called George, I believe, but no one called him so now. He was of a size that could politely be described as considerable. To see his large figure labouring along the street leaning sideways against the weight of his camera bag, you wondered why he didn't take up an undemanding office job where work and retirement weren't too dissimilar.

Zoom had once been a good photographer, lean and quick with a slippery mind and endearing young charms. He had been a favourite of picture editors of daily metropolitans, and for that earned himself some plum assignments. Having seen his portfolio I realised he had obviously been a craftsman – skilled not only in technique but sympathetic of mood, alert to opportunity and, above all, supremely lucky.

Lesser types used to latch on to him at assignments. They followed wherever he went, they raised their cameras when he did, and pressed their shutters in unison – thinking less of the scene in the frame than of the photographer beside them. Zoom used to play games with them, especially those equipped with fancy motor-drive units capable of shooting many frames per second. With these he would cry wolf, raising his camera with a startled rush but not firing... He figured they'd be the ones who'd have to face their picture editors to explain the rolls and rolls of nondescript exposed film.

He had been, I believe, a lad and a larrikin, blessed with puckish mischief and winning ways. Politicians he persuaded into most unpolitic situations, and with his cameras he reduced the famous to the most common denominator. Everyday life he captured in its glory and its fragility. His action shots were history caught and held in time. He had clearly lived on the run. Nosy, perhaps bullish, not to be dissuaded, he had forged his reputation. His exploits were legendary.

One of his tales involved the chief photographer on one of his past papers. Like many men of the press, he hated a beer, and had an arrangement that each night he'd get a lift with Zoom past the Imperial. Zoom would slow down the car, the photographer would open the door, grab his camera bag and dash off between the lines of traffic into the warm and comforting confines of the saloon bar.

'One night, there we were in the car, and as usual I slow down in the stream of traffic for this bloke to hop out. But – bugger me dead if I haven't got to his bag earlier, drilled through the base of it and into the floor of the car and bolted them together. Oh, I still remember it as he bolted out in the Godalmighty rush – only to be whipped back by a bag that wouldn't move.' He laughed, wiping the tears from the creases at the corners of his eyes.

'And of course I have to keep up with the traffic, so I put my foot down and speed up. And there he is, flapping alongside the car, yelling and waving and looking stupid. Cursing enough to turn the air purple. Took a dislike to me after that. No sense of humour.

Zoom lasted eleven years in daily papers and that was eleven years multiplied many times over in most people's lives. And it meant he survived long enough to leave, but only just.

The story went that the decline started when his wife left him. 'If you can ignore a woman long enough she will discover she doesn't need you,' said Zoom. 'Show her apology, show her anger, even show her a fist, and she will stay. But ignore her and she won't.'

This could have been insight or hindsight. The fact was his wife left and Zoom was launched over the edge. Loneliness and a lifetime of drink wrought their changes. His quicksilver spirit dulled and his inspiration just dribbled away. He became one of the shelly-backs to be found in all the press pubs around the big cities. It was only a matter of time before he was chewed up and spat out by the newspaper game, crushed under its daily juggernaut.

'And I was replaced by a cadet. Can you believe that?' he

would say. 'A bloody cadet with acne and chin fluff you could see daylight through.'

I had known too many Zooms to show much sympathy.

He must have gone under for a time, probably spanning his days between the pubs and the cheap, damp lodgings where washed-up hacks go to die. But somehow he managed to surface and land the job at this paper. He had been at the *Weekly Advertiser* so long that his past was almost another life, like the Dreamtime of Aboriginal legend. When he spoke of it he made it sound like a gambol through the Elysian Fields — not really there but a shadowy memory of what had been there.

A slow and reluctant worker, keen only to get the easiest shot possible, his photographs were uninspired and occasionally bad. He was here because he had nowhere else to go. His working days ranged from one mundane shot to another, and he travelled between assignments in a battered old car that was his mobile wardrobe and drinks cupboard. The floor of the car was a carpet of empty beer bottles and used matches. And at night, he never entered Molloy's – preferring, as all defeated souls, to irrigate his sadness in private.

Today, there was a worried air about Zoom as he came into my office. It was not the look of a man suffering from the indulgences of the previous night – Zoom had a built-up immunity to that. The look on his face and all about him was one of consternation, and it was one of the rare times he showed an emotion other than fatigue. He rested his ample bulk in a chair. 'Got a moment?'

'Sure.'

'Got a story, I think.'

This was something most unusual. 'What's it about, Zoom?'

He scratched the back of his hand and looked around the room. When he spoke, it was with his eyes frozen to a point on the wall slightly to the left of me. 'It could be a hard story. It's touchy. But I've got the photographs to prove it, you can see it all from them.'

'Go on.'

'I picked up this story from . . . from someone around the place who was telling me about this kid, a young boy, whose parents keep him chained up like an animal. They reckoned that this couple keep this kid chained up like a prisoner in the house and bash him – they've heard his screams. Sometimes he's chained up in the back yard of the house for most of the day, in all weathers.'

'How long has this been going on?'

'Months, they say. And the kid's been getting worse and worse, all covered in blood and bruises. There's never been anything like a doctor or a social worker or anything like that around the place. And they just keep beating the living daylights out of this kid.'

'Have they told the police?'

'Reckon they don't want to look like sticky-beaks.'

'But they're willing to let us be.'

'Looks that way.'

'You say you've got pictures?'

He pulled out a wad of photographs. 'I called around there early one afternoon last week and had a peek over the fence. He was there all right, poor little bugger.' It was the first time I had heard Zoom express pity for anyone other than himself. The photographs were moving. Sitting among the tussocks of grass in an unkempt garden was the crumpled figure of a child. The manacles on his feet were clearly visible, as were the heavy chains linked to a metal post.

'But I couldn't get him to turn and face me. I tried calling and whistling but he was just slumped there, you know, hardly moving. So I wacked on a long lens and got that close-up.' The gangly arms and legs of the child were mottled with bruises. 'I reckoned that was almost proof enough.'

'Do many people know about this?'

'There's probably a lot more people know about it as haven't said so.'

'But this is child-bashing. This is cruelty.'

'I know that but . . . well, people are funny around here.'

'Haven't any of these people spoken to the parents?'

'Reckon they've hardly seen the parents since they moved in. There's a mother comes in and out occasionally, but no one's seen her around town. Father must be unemployed, they've only seen him once and it seems he sits inside for most of the day. No one knows them. They haven't spoken to a soul.'

'Seems very odd.'

'Yes, I know, but this place is always throwing up surprises.'

'Whereabouts is this house?'

27

He mentioned the name of the street, one of the tracks I knew of at the outskirts of town where ramshackle houses scattered themselves idly between clumps of grey-green bush.

'The place hasn't got a street number, but it's a run-down old weatherboard place, needs a paint, with a green front door and a high fence around the rear garden,' said Zoom.

'I suppose it's worth a look.'

'I'd say so,' said Zoom. 'Do you like the pictures?'

'Yes,' I said. 'Since you asked. Yes.'

The house appeared deserted. I knocked at the green door several times but got no answer. I pushed it gently. It opened and, trying to look casual, I walked inside. I wondered how many pairs of eyes were watching from behind the net curtains of other windows.

The lounge-room was small and in a clutter of old and tired furniture. Washing left to dry in front of the radiator had been pulled away and scattered around the room. There were cheap prints of tree-framed sunsets on the walls and a pink, heavy-fringed shade on the lamp standing in the corner. Several children's toys were strewn across the floor. The squares of carpet laid down in a jigsaw of differing colours and patterns were stained here and there. The paint had been chipped from the walls in places and there were two big holes in the plaster.

It looked like there had been a fight in here, or at least a struggle.

The kitchen at one end of the room was a shamble of unwashed dishes and discarded food. A chair was overturned. Spillages down the sides of the cupboards had become smeared with sticky fingerprints. It seemed as if the characters in a chaotic household had rushed away from the pandemonium without stopping to clear aside the mess. I felt like the man who discovered the *Marie Celeste*.

Further along the passage I found the child's darkened bedroom. The boy had obviously struggled hard, spilling out of his bed in the fight and dragging the blankets with him across the floor as he fought and twisted. Opening the curtains I saw the clutter of broken toys underfoot, the long scratches on the paintwork of the walls and, most evil sight of all, four cords tied to each of the bed's corners.

I wondered what sort of torture went on here. I wondered what sort of sickness had set itself in the minds of the parents.

Perhaps they were religious freaks intent on thrashing some imagined devil out of the child's body. Perhaps they were violent and dissolute drunks. Perhaps they were just very sick people.

Then I remembered the father, the shadowy figure never seen to leave the house. I spun around. The room was empty. I edged up to the door, alert to the faintest sound of another body. I looked cautiously down the hall, fearing to see some bull-necked study of mad rage waiting to attack. There was none. The rest of the house sounded empty. I walked slowly, lowering each step to the floor and wrapping myself close to the walls through the kitchen and into the lounge-room.

The door to the main bedroom was closed. It looked more solid and more threatening as I moved closer. The blood was pumping through me as I felt for the handle and turned it.

If he wasn't asleep, if he was awake, he would spring at me the moment the door opened. I flattened myself tight against the wall and slowly pushed the door with one hand. It moved further and further and there seemed to be no sound coming from the room. I looked around the back of the door, expecting some looming hulk of a man wound up taut for the attack. There was none.

The room, like the rest of the house, was small and undistinguished, with sallow green walls clashing with the orange carpet. There were pictures of ballerinas on the walls, the sort of pictures a woman would hang. It was most assuredly a woman's bedroom, with its net curtains, the white wardrobe and the discarded clothes over the single bed.

'What do you think you're doing here?'

A low female voice turned me on my heels. It was a soft voice and I felt guilty for more reasons than I could think of.

'What are you doing here? Are you from the department?'

'No.' I staggered out with the words. 'From the paper.'

She hardly seemed to register what I said. 'That's all right then. Do you want a cup of coffee?'

I nodded, dumb with embarrassment. It was as if she accepted the presence of a reporter in her house, in her bedroom. 'I'm from the *Weekly Advertiser*,' I offered, following her into the kitchen.

She just nodded, filling the kettle and setting it on the stove.

'Some people suggested I come around to see you.'

Again she nodded, dropping spoonfuls of coffee into the cups.

'It's about your son, I believe.'

The spoon slowly went down to the bench top. The kettle gurgled away in the sudden silence around the room. She looked away and stood very still. A small, stringy woman, maybe not yet thirty, she did not give the appearance of a violent ogre. She gave a tired sigh. 'What about Tim?'

'Your son.' I took a breath. 'There's been complaints. People have been seeing what's been happening here.'

She turned to face me, and I saw her mouth tighten and her thin-plucked eyebrows draw together. 'Meddling bloody so-and-sos,' she muttered, her voice soft and frighteningly quiet.

'Why do you say that?'

'Why don't they keep their bloody noses out of other people's business?'

'Can you blame them?'

'Of course I can.' She whirled away with ferocity. 'It's nothing to do with them . . . or you. Nothing in the world.'

'But what you're doing . . .'

'What I'm doing? What about that mob of tell-tales out there? What about them? What about that bloody bunch of do-gooding bastards?'

'But what about your son?'

'What's it got to do with you? You're not his father.'

'Where is his father?'

'Dunno.'

'I just don't know how you've got away with it for so long. The screaming and the scratches and the mess of this place. Leaving the poor kid trussed up like that. I tell you now – we've got photos to prove it – don't you worry about that. We've got you good and proper. You're not fit to be human, you or that husband of yours.'

'I haven't any husband . . .'

'That man who came here with you.'

'That's not his father. That's not my husband. He don't even live here. So you just tell those sticky-arses out there that they're wrong. It's just Tim and me here.'

'You mean to say that . . . that everything that goes on here is just you?'

'Of course. His dad shot through.'

'And I don't blame him. You need a psychiatrist, and that poor kid of yours needs to be taken away from you as soon as possible.'

'Oh, they all said that.'

'And now I see why.'

'And how would you know? How would you know what it's like trying to cope with a kid like that?'

'So it's the kid's fault, is it? It's all the kid's fault, I suppose.'

'Of course it's not the kid's fault. God help me, it's no one's fault. It's fate, or genes, or something – I don't know.'

'What are you getting at?'

'Well, the poor little bugger couldn't help the way he turned out, could he? And we'd never had it in the family before. It was nothing hereditary, this autism. Christ, I don't think I'd even heard of it until he was born. And the first time they told me, the first time I realised . . . hell, I just didn't know what to think.'

'Your kid's autistic?'

'And hyperactive. It wears me out completely, I tell you. It was all right when he was younger and smaller. I could handle him then. But he's grown so big and heavy. I just can't control him when he gets going. He's stronger than three of me.'

'So how do you cope?'

'You manage somehow, don't you,' she said, fishing through her pockets for a cigarette.

'What about social welfare, don't they help you out?'

She drew heavily on her cigarette, flicked back her head and exhaled a long, angry cloud of smoke. 'Christ almighty, if I let any of those bastards in here . . .' She looked around the room, raking her hand through her hair and shaking her head.

'Have you ever hit him?'

'I suppose I have, once or twice. Perhaps more. But nothing bad. And only when things get too much for me, I guess. It gets to me after a while, it just turns me. If I leave him inside all day he just wrecks the place when I'm not here. But I can't keep running backwards and forwards from work to pick up his mess and see he's not in trouble. I've just got to keep him tied up when I'm not here.'

'You work?'

'At the fruit cannery at Tingalla.'

'Why on earth do you work?'

'We've got to live, Tim and me. His father did the midnight flit up to Queensland somewhere and stopped paying maintenance. They never traced him.'

'Can't you live on the dole?'

'Single mum's payment? And besides, if I registered, they'd find me.'

'You mean you're hiding?'

'That's why I moved up here.' She gave a long sigh. 'They were wanting to put Tim in a home. That was all very well, but the only place they could fit him in was a home way across the other side of the state. I don't have much money. I don't even have a car. There'd be no way in the world that I could have gone over to see him once a month, much less once a week. And I wanted to see him more than that. I wanted to have him close to me. I don't know why, but I do.' She stubbed out her cigarette. 'Anyway, I told them that and then they turn around – oh, it was some toffy woman in the department; some stuck-up bitch in pearls – and she told me the only other place close to Melbourne was this other home that sometimes has spare beds because it was really an old people's place. Sometimes they'd bring in a kid if one of those old vegetables died. And she tells me I've no option, and if I didn't make a decision the department would make it for me. I didn't know what to do. The thought of putting him into that old people's place – I tell you, it put the chills in me, leaving Tim in some place like that . . .'

'And so you came up here to hide?'

'What else could I do? It was the only thing open to me – or else they'd take him away from me. And if I know anything, I know I didn't want that.'

'Do you still think that?'

'More than ever.'

Her gaze wandered across the kitchen. 'Oh shit, it's starting to rain. I've got to get him inside. Could you give me a hand?'

The first heavy raindrops were slashing a path down the windows. She ran out into the garden, and there I saw the slumped mass of the child. Unloosing the binds, she strained at his weight, trying to lift him to his feet. I joined her, and only then realised what a weight a child could be.

We dragged him inside the house and into his room, dodging his flailing arms and legs, and hoisted him on to the bed. She grabbed and tied one of his wrists. 'If I don't do this he'll probably roll out of bed again and scream merry hell,' she said, still panting. 'Last week he pulled the wardrobe down on to himself.'

He was making loud grunts and starting to thrash around on the bed, striking at the headboard with his knuckles. I grabbed the free wrist and tied it with the rope, realising only afterwards what I had done. I looked up. Kneeling by the bedside, she was stroking the mad, troubled mass of his hair and making quiet, lulling noises. He wrenched and struggled for a time until, slowly transfixed by the sound and the sight of her face, he lay still.

The pair of them ignored me as I watched, wishing to hell that I had a camera now and thinking all the while that there were times when even the camera lies.

Tam

There was a man in my kitchen. He hung his weight on the refrigerator door, convincing himself that the remains of last night's dinner were truly dead. Around his legs a cat danced a slow pirouette of hunger. They were, the pair of them, complete strangers to me.

Living out on the plains at Griggs's old place meant I rarely had company. Some of the cattle agisted in the nearby home paddock made forays into the yard after trampling the old wire-strand fence. Sometimes a farm cat passed through on a hunting prowl. A fertiliser salesman dropped in, but then, so did an insurance salesman. You can never be too far away from civilisation.

The man in my kitchen sighed and shut the door of the refrigerator, sending the cat skittering past me and out of the door.

'That's Samovar.' He spoke over his shoulder as he opened each cupboard in turn, looking for something to eat. 'Russian Blue – very friendly breed.'

It had been a long, tedious day, drawn out by the unseasonal and incessant grey drizzle. At least the intruder had warmed up the house by the time I got home. The piles of newspapers I had been saving to read at leisure were roaring red and orange in the fire.

'Excuse me,' I ventured. 'Are you a burglar?'

'Not now. Gave it up years ago. There was no money in it,' he said, picking up a half-eaten crust of cold toast and chewing it. He scratched at a pimple on his chin and looked around at the uneasy disorder of the kitchen. 'Name's Tam,' he said, picking up another crust and chewing that.

'Why are you here?'
'Live here.'
'Do you?'
'Moved in today. You?'
'I... er... I live here too,' I said nonchalantly. Stunned, really. Old man Griggs hadn't told me he'd rented out the spare room. Still, he hadn't said he wouldn't.

And Tam had indeed moved in. The spare room was now a bedroom of distinction. A rumpled mattress spilled bedclothes across the floor. Clothes lay about in defeated heaps, save a suit hanging from the mantelpiece. Shouldering for space were cardboard boxes spewing out books and papers. Walls once bare now carried a large and gaudy painting of the Sacred Heart in a chipped ornate frame. Someone had added fangs and demonic eyebrows in felt pen on the glass. Wetted beer-bottle labels had been stuck in the shape of a cross on the wall over the mattress. How all this had happened I had no idea. He appeared to have neither a car nor a house-key. When I came back to the kitchen he had disappeared.

'Gone drinking with intent,' said the note pencilled blackly on the kitchen table. 'Back soon.'

I really didn't need Tam, or his cat, or the budgie I discovered swinging crazily in its cage hung up on the shower rail.

I never questioned how Tam made a living – it never seemed the right sort of question. His skin was too white for him to be working outdoors, and his hours too irregular for him to be an office worker. He didn't buy food, but every so often he turned up trumps with a side of lamb or a box of vegetables, the origins of which I knew never to question.

Small and simian, he had a body that was angular and eyes that seemed to have withdrawn into their hollows. He slept a lot, he barely ate, and there seemed to be his own personal Fury inside him – trapped and battering to be loosed.

One day I found him strutting around the house wearing a folded paper hat on which he had written 'Stetson – grey with red feather'. Another time I found him sitting naked at the kitchen table with a piece of string around his neck. Tied to the string was a paper tag which read, 'Bow tie and tails'.

He certainly spent a lot of time in his room painting, an activity that a man doesn't admit to in this part of the world.

His paintings were large and frenetic, slashed through with colour and full of fractured images.

He showed me one – a naked woman playing percussion. 'I call it Sex Cymbal,' he said. I laughed, and he never showed me another painting.

When it rained, he hung his washing on a rope he strung across the hall. Entering the house was like walking into a festoon of flags. The dripping clothes swamped the hall carpet. It was like crossing a sodden paddock. Once he threw a red singlet into my soaking shirts. I had to go to work looking like I had sustained some serious wound to my left shoulder.

His own clothes were oddments of questionable age and dubious elasticity, and mostly long due for the rag bag. Threadbare remnants of underpants were more like webbing held together by tired elastic, and yet he clung to them all with an animal tenacity.

I found him dangling some seaweed into the budgie's cage.

'I'm trying to make him vegetarian,' he said.

'But he already is. He eats bird seed.'

'No, I fed him mince last week. I'm afraid I might have got him addicted. The week before I fed him cheese and it plugged up his bowels. Birds are very delicate.'

Then, one Sunday morning, I found my car was missing.

I woke up Tam. 'Have you seen my car?'

'Yes, I borrowed it last night. You'd fallen asleep in front of the fire.'

'And?'

'The fire went out.'

'And the car?'

'Dunno. Haven't seen it since. Did you say you were making coffee?'

I sat heavily on the edge of his mattress. 'Did you come back with the car?'

'Could you put a slug of brandy in my coffee?' he said, rolling away from me.

'You mean it was stolen?'

'Well, I couldn't see it. Oh, I forgot, I drank the last of the brandy yesterday.'

'But you borrowed my car . . .'

'Hmm.'

'And you lost it.' My voice was starting to edge into falsetto. 'Where did you leave it?'

'Dunno. Outside a pub. A pub. Somewhere.'

'Molloy's?' It was like extracting a very tough tooth.

'Can't remember.'

'You forgot where you left it?' I was starting to strain at the collar. 'Isn't that a bloody stupid thing to do?'

'Yeh. Had to walk home. Took me hours. Didn't you say you were making coffee?'

Wordless from sheer rage, I thumped into the kitchen, put on the kettle and walked out of the house – leaving the whistling water to scream out my frustration.

There was another bottle of brandy. Wise to Tam's weakness, I had hidden it from him, and recovered it that night after I heard him go out. Where he was going, I couldn't say, and didn't much care. I cared even less as I pulled more of the bottle. We had not spoken all day since the morning – and I didn't care much about that, either.

Warmed by the alcohol, I took the bottle far out into the paddock, sat on a stump and watched the night.

The pale gravel of the track lay silent, silvered by the moonlight. It stretched far away to the flat line of the horizon, a single thread lying over countless thousands of acres, beyond which lay yet more countless thousands of acres. And all of them spanned across by other pale, silvered gravel tracks. And then I saw the curved side of the earth criss-crossed by a whole network of gravel tracks that led into towns, where they became tarmac roads, and thence on to cities where they widened under strings of brilliant arc-lights: white, blue, orange. And then they led into the hub of clustered neon forests and out again to the towns before dwindling back to pale tracks pushing further into the blackness.

The fragility of it against the enormity of the dark earth – I sat silent and could not think any more.

Through the thick haze of morning sleep, I heard the sound of movement outside my window. The warm wind pushing in also carried the sound of Tam shifting and shuffling in the toilet. Parked outside the toilet was a car, gleaming, lustrous and rust-free. It made me wake quickly.

I found Tam painting crabs on the toilet seat.

'Yeh,' said Tam, stopping to wipe his paintbrush on his trousers. 'Figured you needed a car.'

'You didn't buy it, did you?'

'No.' He was concentrating on mixing his paint into a vivid lime green.

'Well, where did you get it?'

'Dunno.'

'It's expensive. It's almost new.'

'Is it? Then it should have been locked up,' he said, washing his brush with a flush of the toilet. 'Don't use the seat for a while, would you. Got to let the paint dry.'

Jack Mollison

Jack Mollison was once said to be the best forward yet produced by the town. The team he captained won successive finals for no fewer than six years and included a memorable game where eight players were transported to the hospital in varying degrees of bloodied pulp. Jack was not among them.

He had a fist the size of a small melon. He could flex a bicep of twenty inches around even before the season's training started. In form, he had been seen lifting single-handed a sheep in full wool and carrying it over his shoulder across the paddocks. Deep and barrel-chested, with great oaks for thighs, he was not only the strongest man around the district but had a talent to shift that bulk around the field at quicksilver speed. To hear the tales of his sporting feats you'd think he was Atlas. Nijinsky and Houdini rolled into one. And so he probably was.

But all that was more than twelve years ago, and, time being the heartless beast it is, he now stood a sad relict of the glorious days. The tone of those great muscles had slackened, and the proud protrusion of his chest had subsided into a soft rounding of the gut. Countless glasses of beer had passed through him, and he had a legacy of knee injuries that put him beyond hard physical slog.

The fact that he had not been snapped up by a major metropolitan team and taken to Melbourne was indeed a sad thing. Far sadder, however, was the fact that he had stayed in this part of the world. People knew of his lost strength, and for them strength was a matter of reverence.

Every time they gathered at Molloy's front bar to recall the last great era of the town's team, the presence of Jack Mollison was made sadder. It was cruelty that knew no respite, and I sometimes worried that the passing friendship I had with the man was born of pity. Perhaps it was.

It struck me that the public scorn he suffered sprang from the peculiar morality of these parts. He was certainly a drinker, and a hard one to beat. But it was figured that a man owed it to himself to drag himself out of a hole. His mates were there to help him, but first he had to show the battling spirit. Weak wills did not deserve help. I could imagine the women clucking their tongues and shaking their heads, and the men holding their silence.

He was never a happy drunk. He was just a drunk: a sad, stumbling, hang-dog inebriate. And if ever I felt sorry for him, it was on the night of his death.

Jack Mollison died without glory and amid a great deal of mess. I saw him under the arc-lights set up by the roadside. It was like someone had put his guts into a paper bag and dashed it furiously against the tarmac of the highway. There was little of him that was identifiable, all slashed through with skewers of metal and glass and the vital organs split open under the swirling light of the ambulance and police car.

I'd been called to help identify him, and came from Molloy's where, half an hour previously, I'd seen him leave. Like the rest of the crowd, I noticed him nod his nightly farewell before turning back to my beer. It seemed no one in particular talked to him; they more acknowledged him. They did not ask if he was fit enough to drive home. He had been there since opening time. But then, he was most days, and it had never stopped him getting his car home before. He sometimes offered lifts to people, proving to them in some way, if not to himself, that he was capable of controlling a car. And it was on this night – perhaps for the first time – that someone accepted.

Those that saw it happen said later they thought the kid was having him on. Some sort of joke, they thought. He was one of the youngest Printz boys and had just started his apprenticeship at his father's shop. He still had to establish himself at Molloy's. They thought he was joking, and no one noticed him leave after accepting Mollison's offer. Even if they had noticed, I doubt anyone would have done anything.

The kid was not unconscious when I got there, but lay whimpering softly with his arms and legs skewed into impossible angles. He had been fortunate, thrown clear before the shattered engine flew backwards into the cabin of the car, crushing it tight from firewall to back seat. Projected through the windscreen, he became a missile, landing on the fuel-sprayed road, sliding and rolling more than sixty feet from where the wreck finally stopped.

It appeared he had been not just fortunate, but very fortunate. The shattered glass had not sliced his neck but only cut through the skin of his face and shoulders, where spattered blood was starting to cake brown. The blood around him still glowed dimly in the urgent lights.

The car lay steaming and jagged. Skid marks went back more than two hundred feet, weaving wildly from one splay of gravel verge to the other. Showers of glass and metal littered the road. The boot had sprung open to reveal several boxes of beer bottles still intact and waiting to be drunk. And from underneath the seat, which was sodden with Jack's blood, a fireman pulled out the fragments of a rum bottle, still smelling of its contents.

During the mop-up, men would suddenly leave, and I could hear the private sounds of dry retching away in the dark. The boy, they said, may not be paralysed. And plastic surgeons may be able to pull his face back together again, at least to make him look human, they said.

Jack, in the cruelty of it all, had been very much the luckier of the pair.

Days later, I was driving far out on the plains and passed a tiny, one-roomed school. The class was outside, and I could see the small boys playing football. They played with lop-sided grace and unkillable energy born of dreams of stardom with the local firsts. And Jack Mollison had once been a kid kicking a football barefoot around the dry yellow oval of some remote rural school.

I planted my foot and pushed the car faster and faster along the road. And as I drove the tears came.

Day of the Carrot

Ruling this town was a fraternity, a Broederbond of sorts, comprising men of power and time to enact and enforce the codes of behaviour needed to keep such a small, concentrated settlement on an even keel. They were the same names that appeared on the membership lists of the football club and the cricket club, the RSL and the Red Cross. They were all members of the golf club and all Rotarians. Their wives, universally beefy, bossy and loud-voiced, ran the women's memberships of the same organisations.

As a group they collected a disproportionate number of the MBE and OBE awards handed out each year in the Queen's Birthday Honours list. You couldn't deny they worked hard for their awards, although an observer may note that their efforts were sprung from the eventual aim of receiving one.

I wondered if their close friendships with Hegarty were necessarily a good thing. Take old man Tilson, for example. Hegarty had frequent dealings with him, and I sometimes thought the garage owner might have more of a stake in the paper than I knew.

These were my idle thoughts as I returned to the office one afternoon after yet another marvellous lunch at Molloy's. Hegarty came into my office, bringing with him such a threatening mien I wondered which of the town heavies he'd been speaking to.

'Tell me what you've been writing about lately,' he said. I felt Tilson's hand, black with sump oil, touch the back of my neck in a half-nelson. It was obviously the story in last week's paper.

'One of the best stories,' I started, 'and the one that everyone commented on, was the story of the foul-up at the Council pool.'

'Go on.'

'Well, it was just before the pool opened a fortnight ago that the workmen put the chlorine in the water . . .'

'Yes.'

'And because the water was still, and because they hadn't been able to fill the pool entirely, and because the supplier didn't have any dosage charts or instruction leaflets to give them, they put too much in. It irritated a lot of the kids' eyes and brought up some skin problems. They had to empty all the water and refill the pool. And with water being scarce . . .'

'Who was the supplier?'

The only supplier in town was Tilson. As I spoke, I tried to choke back his name.

Hegarty sat back. 'Good story,' he said. 'Very good.'

It threw me utterly. I had been sure Tilson would have taken a slice off him for that story.

'And what else have you written?'

'There was the annual general meeting of the hospital?'

He nodded. 'Well written.'

'And the football club presentations?'

'Nicely handled. Like the picture.'

'The RSL bingo night?'

He just kept smiling and nodding. I was running out of suggestions. The Council, the hospital, the football club – what was there left to stir the anger of the editor?

'The CWA prayer meeting, and the special appeal they launched?' I offered. If only he would stop looking so pleased with me. I was sweating visibly. 'Yes, and there was the story about the Fire Brigade's summer warnings, the agriculture department bit on supplementary feeding, that big carrot grown by the kid Willis, the tennis marathon for the high-school kids, a statement from the Post Office about . . .'

'The carrot grown by the kid Willis. The two-foot carrot grown by the kid Willis. Well, well,' he said.

If ever I had felt the earth shifting as I walked, now was that time. I tried to comprehend, but comprehension just wouldn't come. I couldn't understand the cause of Hegarty's displeasure. A carrot, after all, is a carrot. Who could have taken offence at that? Had I got the kid's name wrong? Had his father really grown it? Or his aunt? Or the neighbour five miles down the road who hadn't realised it had gone missing from the vegetable garden? Had he used growth hormones still classified as a government secret?

'A carrot, eh?'

'About two feet long,' I said.

'And tell me – why did you do a story like that?'

'For a bit of light relief, I guess. Something to lift the paper a bit. And because it was unusual.'

He nodded thoughtfully. 'Let's take a walk.'

He led me to the door and walked me around the presses as he spoke. 'I've just been called to Martha's front counter to see a woman, a very forceful lady and one capable of physical feats barely believable for one of her sex. And she has a pumpkin, a very big pumpkin. And she feels that – since we printed a story and a photograph of little Willis's big carrot – her pumpkin deserves one too.'

'I see,' I said, relieved. 'To keep her happy we'll just get the photo and run it in a few weeks' time.'

Hegarty had been steering me towards his office. 'That's an interesting idea,' he said. 'But what are you going to do with this lot here, then?'

He opened the door to his office. There were onions stretched the length of the floor; a mushroom the size of a footstool; a cabbage of indecent size and shape nudged up to some huge pink blooms and a handful of some overblown sprouts. A jar, containing a dead spider floating in spirits was surrounded by dried pea-pods the length of a man's forearm. And a two-headed lizard was trapped beneath an upturned wire bin.

'It's been Covent Garden in here while you were at lunch. A real Harvest Festival without the hymns. I've completely exhausted my vocabulary of superlatives. I can't think when I last enjoyed myself so much. Perhaps I should change the sign out the front to "Weekly Advertiser and Costermongers". I could diversify my business interests, couldn't I?' He was standing so close to me that our noses almost touched.

'I really didn't realise . . .'

'I know you didn't realise. Funny, isn't it.' He turned away from me. I breathed out. 'And now, about this pumpkin. Perhaps we could get photos of it. Perhaps we could get photos of all of these and run them in a weekly column. We could call it "Freaks". Do you like that name? After all, these people will be expecting some mention in the paper. After all, there was that carrot...'

He drifted off, looked over the scene and shook his head. 'This afternoon you are going to clear out this mess. You will return each item to its rightful owner and think up some plausible excuse why it will not appear in print. But before you do that, you are going to break the news to Madame Pumpkin, who is still waiting – and has been waiting for some time – at the front counter. You will go and break the news to her and what she then breaks... well... there are band-aids behind Martha's desk.'

The Call to Freedom

Glasses were swilled silently that afternoon in Molloy's. Cigarettes were lit wordlessly and smoked despondently. The crowd that had gathered at the front bar scuffed their feet on the linoleum and watched as they did so. Not one man looked up as Freedom read from the letter he held.

Freedom was the sort of man who usually held boisterous court in the front bar. It was his second office and his second home. As the town plumber he was widely known, and for his nickname he was even more widely known. The name had come from some friend who once bellowed across the front bar, 'For Chrissakes, give us Freedom from Unger.' And for Jim Unger the name 'Freedom' was born. He was a popular man, known to knock down the price of a plumbing job for a pensioner or a farmer in a bad season. And he enjoyed a certain public respect for the way he prepared the RSL hall each Anzac Day for the commemoration service. It was his year's work rolled into a frenetic six hours as he directed Council workmen delivering plants to decorate the stage, setting up a sound system for the traditional address and bringing in the boxes and boxes of beer for everyone's enjoyment.

The day before Anzac Day he traditionally spent cleaning the hall, and the night before he would set the alarm clock and radio to start the day with the dawn service broadcast from the Melbourne Shrine.

Mrs Unger had her yearly task of pressing his blue suit, worn only for funerals and Anzac Day. But for weeks before she and the other women had been busily baking for the luncheon. The creations of those kitchens were airy confections of egg and flour spread through with jam and dusted with sugar or served with a liberality of cream. It was scarcely food for an army parade, more for a fashion parade. There was something slightly ludicrous in the sight of whipped cream smeared over the face of an avowed steak-and-chips man. There was something distasteful in the sight of it all being washed down with draughts of beer. That so many of those dainty sweetmeats should be found regurgitated into the gutter was a secret known only to the cleaners who came through early the following morning.

Being a solemn occasion, it was unseemly to consider the day as an extravagant booze-up. But it was just as unseemly to finish the day without having to crawl along the gutter in the general direction of home.

Like many country towns, this place had experienced the patriotic fervour that swept through the country in the wake of 1914–18. And in that sweeping nationalism was bestowed on every town, no matter how small, a welter of statuary to honour the war and its victims. Mostly it was a downcast soldier, hands resting on a rifle butt and head bowed in stony memory of dead local lads. Country areas had been particularly generous in that war. Strapping country lads, eager-eyed for adventure beyond the horizons of yellowed paddocks, offered themselves and their horses in days when mounted rifles were regular fare for the adventures of boys' books. And in their departure the hopes of more fathers and more farms than ever could be imagined withered. I had always thought it odd that these towns chose statues of foot soldiers, but I suppose one of a mounted infantryman would have cost a good deal more.

In this town, however, public subscriptions gathered after the war warranted a statue of distinction. They collected enough funds to buy an angel mounted on a stone plinth in the grassed area in front of the weatherboard RSL hall. It was a sorrowing creature with outspread wings and holding a wreath. Local wits had dubbed it the 'Dirty Angel' because, when seen askance, the position of its hand and the protrusion of the wreath gave it the appearance in profile of enjoying very public self-abuse. It was never mentioned too widely, however, this being a patriotic place where the Union Jack was still flown on special occasions.

The spirit was revived each year. Medals were brought out of boxes and polished up for the Anzac Day parade down Federation Street to the RSL. Tales of wartime high jinks were revived and retold in detail in Molloy's. Mick Molloy happened to like Anzac Day, for it meant sizeable sales and kept the books up at a normally slack time of year.

Molloy looked the most worried of all the silent men listening as Freedom read haltingly from the letter. He read as if he held a hope that the words would magically change on repeated reading. It was no use. The words sat black and crisp on the sheet of paper bearing the Shire Council crest.

'The wedding reception booked for April 25 is from 1.30 p.m. to 11 p.m. Usual requirements apply, including the arrangements of cleaning and attendance by hallkeeper Mr J. Unger during the reception and to secure the hall afterwards.

'The Shire Council note the traditional use of the hall by the RSL on this day, but also noted the fact that this had been a hitherto informal arrangement. The applicants lodged the necessary form PHB/35 on March 3, so overriding any informal use that had existed previously. Signed – P. Maddocks, Shire Secretary, Shire of Nooweep.'

His voiced trailed off. He stared at the paper as if his gaze could erase the words. There was a long silence. Pam the barmaid slipped away to tell the news to the women in the ladies' lounge. The silence stretched onwards, and then, to a man, a cry of protest went up. It was a noisy and inflamed anger that swelled through the room and out of the windows. It surged up from the pub, way down Federation Street and well into the night.

A stranger stopping in the town may perhaps have wondered which dead-set favourite had failed to make it home in the straight.

The day was as bitter as you could never hope for on that Anzac Day, and the very sky itself seemed to be brooding. Fat clouds rose on the heat from the earth and hung motionless over the town, refusing to break open. Since dawn it had been like this, when the first visitors trailed antlike into town from across the vastness of the plains. All morning you could pick out from the line of the horizon the funnelling clouds kicked up by their cars. The billows of red dust rose and hung static in the still air long after the car had moved on. They were coming into town from far-distant farms for an annual custom observed as sacred duty.

The town, and the mood of the town, was in shadow. The crowd that gathered did not mill excitedly but stood subdued, slowly drawing together in clusters, drawing apart, gelling again and breaking away. The old soldiers formed ranks and processed down the street, but there was no crispness in their step.

Everyone gathered around the Dirty Angel and stood silent and sullen. Some refused to down-cast their eyes; the older men who stood back, arms folded, were seething and angry as stirred ants. Plates piled with cakes were laid out on trestle tables near by. Women stood over them idly waving away flies from the food. A dog squatted on the hard, dry grass and then made great display of tearing at the ground to bury the mess.

The young Stroud boy was blowing the final notes of the Last Post. 'Lest we forget,' said Dr Forbes. 'Lest we forget,' the crowd replied, and Freedom could be heard clearing his throat. He was looking towards the hall that was to be his particular torture in a short while.

He hadn't taken more then the first few sips of his beer when word came to Molloy's that the caterers had arrived early and wanted to get into the hall. Would Freedom hand over the key?

'Be buggered,' said Freedom. 'Opening time is opening time.' The rest of the front bar concurred.

Word came back to the pub quickly. Unable to find the key to the hall, the caterers had broken in through a side window. Freedom took the news quietly. He slowly drained his glass, set it on the bar and left. The crowd parted, every man watched him and no one said a word. Some things are just too bloody.

Children bare-foot and brown-skinned were running with small yapping dogs at their heels in the wide, open street. Even they fell silent, scuffing at the heat-softened asphalt as Freedom slowly walked past.

The hall was alive by the time he arrived. Pale with fury, he walked into the kitchen. He reeled back. His senses were knocked sideways in the cacophony of noise and the thick steam. He stood there dumbly, mouthing like a fish. More people than he had ever remembered were crowded into the kitchen. Everyone, it seemed, was arguing in high voices in a language he could not understand. With every clang and clatter of cookware the voices rose higher, louder and more unintelligible. Already smells of food swirled around the place, carried away on eddies of steam. Freedom held his breath. He had never smelled food like this before. Huge cauldrons seethed dark liquid, pots spewed over strange green foam and a group of women sat in the corner chattering and fashioning flat rounds of dough with their bare hands.

'Foreign muck. Bloody migrants,' Freedom muttered under his breath. Then he bellowed, 'Now, just hang on a moment here. Stop a minute please. Listen to me. Hang on a moment.'

A man with quick, dark eyes came forward. 'Mr Unger?'

'Yes. Who are you?'

'One moment, please.' The man reached into a bag and handed Freedom a wrapped bottle that felt like Scotch. Expensive Scotch. 'We thank you and hope you enjoy.'

'Well, thank you.' Freedom was suddenly unsure.

'And later perhaps you eat with us? We have much food for people, and you too.'

'Perhaps. We'll see. Later perhaps.' He thought for a moment and, rubbing his face, asked, 'Are you Greeks?'

A shadow passed over the man's face, and he seemed to have to force it clear. 'No, no,' he said. 'Turkish. We are friends of the groom. Family of groom – Adnan – have been here many, many years. They have tomato, pear, orange on good farm back of Tingalla. Irrigation farm and bloody good. And very good soil also, grows very good.' He was steering Freedom to the door. 'We must work now. You come back later, okay? You come back and eat with us? Please. Thank you.'

Freedom found himself nodding, standing outside the kitchen and glad to be holding his wrapped bottle. He was willing to give this mob a go, he thought, turning his back on the explosion of heat and energy behind him and returning to the more traditional hospitality of Molloy's.

The heat of the day swelled into a thick, warm evening. Inside his room off the stage, Freedom spent alternate hours studying the racing forms and watching his small fan slap-slap away at its losing task. The room was close and airless, and Freedom gradually spent more time staring fixedly at the fan as the level of liquid in his Scotch bottle sank lower.

He paid less attention to the sounds coming from the hall. It was filling with people and they all spoke in that same high hubbub. There was the occasional cry of a child, the scraping of chairs and tables, a voice calling out in the strange language, but none of it disturbed his attention from the fan. At first he did not even hear the gentle knock at his door.

It was one of the Printz boys, who tucked his head around the door. 'Mr Molloy sent this,' he said, carrying in a box of beer bottles. 'Figured you deserved it.'

Freedom looked at the bottles. 'And very nice of him too,' he said. 'Could do with a drink. Want some?'

The boy drew up a chair. 'Foreigners out there?'

'Yes, Turks,' said Freedom, handing him a glass.

'Stack of people they've got. Kids too, running around the place like wild things,' the boy said. 'They'll break something if they're not careful.'

Freedom just nodded. He was having to concentrate on listening. He didn't drink Scotch as a rule.

The boy swilled his glass. 'Not right, is it. Them having a party in our hall and us left on the other like that, is it. I mean, it's not as if we haven't a right to use our own hall.'

Freedom nodded slowly. 'Not right at all.'

They drained their glasses. The boy continued. 'And if you think about it, it's a bloody insult. Anzac Day and all that... Gallipoli and what have you. We were fighting the bloody Turks then. Our troops were being slaughtered by them, those Turkish soldiers up on the heights. And now, here they are, whooping it up in our hall, and we're left out in the cold. I tell you, it's not right.'

Freedom stared at the fan.

'Well, got to be going back,' said the boy. 'See you later.'

'Yes,' said Freedom, pulling the top off another bottle.

The first sound of singing cut through his dark thoughts. At first he thought it was the sound of some screaming, injured animal, so high and wild it sounded. It sliced through the hubbub from the hall and wavered just below the threshold of pain. Then it sank through a range of discordant notes like the earthward plummet of a dying blowfly.

Then it came again, higher this time and more penetrating. Freedom moved closer to the door. There was a sudden outburst of noise pulsing out in amplified chaos. It was like a saucepan chorus in the hands of children, an erratic din without melody or harmony to Freedom's ears.

Aghast and startled, he shook his head and moved closer to

the door. There was a primal beat to the drum and a sickening wail to the electric guitars, but he could distinguish nothing else from the thick din rising from the stage next door. Above it all came the searing falsetto of the singer, sounding like someone had taken to his vital parts with a chain-saw. The fluid, unbroken line of pain refused to go away. Freedom listened hard and could not hear the singer stopping to breathe. The deluge of noise rang out loud and incessant and started to turn his nerves.

Freedom walked to the further corner of the room with his hands over his ears. He stood there a moment rocking backwards and forwards trying to block out the noise and trying to will it to stop. It refused. He started to pace the room.

As he walked he swilled from the bottle, and as he drank he thought yet more. The kid was right, he figured. It was an insult to the old soldiers of Suvla Bay and Lone Pine, that's what it was. They may now be dead, but there was still their memory – of course there was. He started talking to himself, his lips moving as he thought. The Turks positioned up on the heights had made mincemeat of the assault, splaying bullets and shells off the beach sands and into the bodies of the AIF troops. He thought of the poor bastards ordered to go over the tops of the trenches and walking chest-first into the wall of fire from the Turkish guns. As they went, they tripped and slid over bodies, still warm and twitching from the last assault. And then their own young bodies were added to the pile. He thought of the men who would have been heroes had they not been cut down. He lost an uncle over there, an older uncle whom he had never met, but his family had talked of him later. Not one of the Gallipoli dead, exactly, but part of that war, and mere matters of detail did not concern him now. The beer fumes and the heat had fermented all logic out of him. His brain was inflamed; his mood never blacker.

The music wound on at a high and rarefied pitch, joined now by heavy stamping and clapping from the hall. He could hear the sounds of breaking glasses and a host of heavy thuds. The floor beneath him shook. There was a crash.

Dropping his bottle he tore open the door and raced on to the stage, dashing straight into the amplifiers.

'Turn this bloody noise down,' he screamed, thrashing about

with the network of leads and wires. 'And get me the hell out of this.'

A tall man made taller by his platform heels and dressed in a shimmering white satin shirt ran over in alarm. The rest of the band rushed in. The long white fringe dangling from the sleeves of the satin shirt caught among the wires and the singer toppled, bringing down sound equipment in a shower of sparks.

Men from the hall started climbing on to the stage. 'Keep your bloody hands off me!' yelled Freedom, struggling to free himself from the wires. He hit out at the hands reaching towards him, he kicked at their shins and rolled free across the edge of the stage and on to the dancers beneath, knocking them down like ten-pins.

A gurgle of screams broke out from the tightly packed crowd. They stampeded away like a thousand skittery bullocks. Freedom lurched headlong into the waves of flesh, trying to batter a breach through.

'Bastards!' he screamed. 'Foreign bastards! Murdering Turkish bastards!' He battered out with his feet and fists. 'This is our hall. Get out of here, all of you.' His brain was spinning, all he could see was a flurry of limbs in a flight of panic. Women fainted, children screamed and in the rush for the doors the fallen were trampled underfoot.

Men tried to grab him. Freedom hit back in wild fury. He grabbed a bottle, smashed it against a table and held up the jagged, broken edge, crouching low like a street fighter. A circle of space widened around him.

'Now, get out of here,' he growled. 'Get out of town – all of you. This is Anzac Day, and don't you ever forget what that means to us.'

Sergeant Lawson shouldered a path through the quietened crowd. He took Freedom's shoulder and gently lifted the bottle out of his hand. 'All right, Freedom, calm down. Let's find somewhere for you to sleep this off.'

Mick Molloy spent the next day polishing his glasses. He held each up to the light, checking for smear marks. 'Tight?' he said, wiping at a glass. 'Tight? Poor old Freedom was tighter than baling twine.'

Budgie Calls

Call it sixth sense, call it intuition. I don't know. There must be more than one reporter who knows a problem call by the way a telephone rings. Something shrill.

I had come to know them as budgie calls, a name derived from the deranged mob of budgie-fanciers who would regularly ring my last paper with news of their latest hatchings or prize-winning bird. Should some raw cub reporter show the slightest interest in their pied sky-blue or opaline olive-green, they would be victim to a host of budgie-breeders demanding similar coverage of their feathered treasures. One lad received so many invitations to budgie shows he had to assume a prolonged and virulent attack of scarlet fever.

It was a Tuesday afternoon, and I had been watching the slow and noisy death of a blowfly spinning on its back along the window sill. There was an insistent tone to the phone's ring and I knew a budgie call was looming large and fearsome. I watched it for a while and then lifted the receiver.

'Newsroom,' I said.

'Can I speak to a reporter?' said a man's voice.

'You have one.'

'Are you a reporter?'

'Yes.'

'Then can I speak to the reporter in charge?'

'I'm the reporter in charge.'

'You're in charge?'

'Yes.'

'Isn't Mr Hegarty in charge?'

'He's the editor. But he doesn't take stories. And he isn't in at the moment.'

'I always thought Mr Hegarty was in charge.'

'Well, he is, but not at the moment. He's out. Maybe I can help you.'

'Can you take down these details and give them to Mr Hegarty?'

'I can do that.'

'Well, I won't give you my name . . .' I laid down my pen and waited for the distant flap of little wings. 'I'm not ashamed to give you my name, you understand, but there are some people in this town . . . and I just don't want my name to appear in print. You make sure of that, now. I'm a respectable citizen and you reporters can do things to a person. Make up things about them. I'm wise to you lot. Don't you even tell Mr Hegarty who phoned.'

'I don't know who you are.'

'Well – that's good then. It's not that I'm ashamed, you understand.'

'What do you want me to tell Mr Hegarty?'

'I've lived in this house for more than forty years. My father, he died from lung cancer in 1952, he spent the last five years of his life in this house and we, the wife and myself, we nursed him through an awful time. Sheer awful.'

'Go on.' The blowfly had now fallen from the sill on to the floor and was kicking out its death rattle against the leg of my desk.

'Now, his father, my grandfather you understand, his father came here from New South Wales and settled here in 1903. Not here, not this very house, but a few miles down the road in the old house before it got burnt. That was in 1927. It was in the paper. I'm sure you'd have it in your files if you wanted to look it up. Elsewise, we have the cutting if you want to drop around some time and have a read of it.'

A right proper budgie.

'He was on the service committee of the RSL. My grandfather and father both served the country – although I was never much one for the RSL. I don't drink – I think you should make note of that. Some of the fellows that get down to the RSL, well, you know what it's like for some people. My father and my grandfather were never anything more than social drinkers and my father worked dashed hard for the RSL. You're not a member of the RSL, are you?'

'No.'

'It's not that I have anything against the RSL, of course. It does a lot of good. But some of the fellows that get down there of a Saturday night . . . well, I don't have to explain it to you.'

'I understand what you're saying.'

'So, we've lived in this place a good many years and it suits the wife and me. We never had no family for one reason or another which I won't go into, and so it's been just the wife and I until this boy turns up, and, honestly, it's just getting the wife down. Her nerves aren't that good. She has shingles and she goes to the doctor's at least every fortnight. It's awful what it's doing to her and I feel so dashed useless about it all.'

'What's upsetting her?'

'It's the boy, you see.'

'Which boy?'

'The boy and all the noise he makes at night. We can't get a wink of sleep, the pair of us. It's shaking up her nerves something dreadful. Really awful.'

'Do you mean some neighbour's boy?'

'I don't know whose boy, whose son. We haven't got any neighbours – not on this part of the road, anyways. And the nearest people, well, we stopped talking to them about ten years back over a bit of a disagreement about the outpaddock.'

'How old is this boy?'

'Dunno. He doesn't seem to do any work. I've never seen him about these parts during the day. It's only at nights. And when he comes in – usually around eleven – he makes that much noise all scrabbling and shuffling about. And the wife's taking fourteen tablets a day for it. It affects her that much.'

The blowfly had finished its death pangs and I had lost interest in it. Now I was hunched over the desk, struggling to make some sense from the words coming down the telephone.

'Is he a lodger with you?'

'All I know is that he doesn't pay nothing to us. And the wife usually takes him up a bit of food most days too.'

'So she's seen him?'

'No.'

'Where does she take up the food?'

'Up into the roof, of course. She just slides a plate of something through the manhole cover up there. Well, I mean, you can't let him starve. It isn't Christian.'

'You have a boy whom you've never seen living in your roof?' I had visions of a thousand fluttering budgies beating against my brain.

'That's right. And he makes a fair old noise about it. Up the drainpipe we hear him of a night. There's a gap in the eaves he must slide through, after shimmying up the drainpipe. He levers himself up on the window sill, we can hear him doing it.'

'He must be fit.'

'I'd say.'

'And so neither of you have seen him or spoken to him?'

'Oh no. He comes in when it's dark, see. You've got no hope of seeing him. But we can hear him all right. He's a cunning one. But he makes a noise and gives us a start something dreadful. I've been to the Council about it, but they've done nothing. They said we should tell him to go to the dole office. And the policeman said he couldn't do anything about it. It's dreadful, I tell you. We're only pensioners and we could do without this.'

'This boy, the one you say lives in your roof' – I realised I was speaking very slowly and clearly – 'what does he do about washing and going to the toilet?'

'Blowed if I know.'

'Does he eat the food?'

'Well, he must. He's still alive.'

'Have you been up there to check?'

'Too dangerous. Can't leave the wife alone. You never know what could happen to her, or me. Now, you might think we're balmy . . .'

'Of course not.'

'But we're not. But I tell you, if it keeps happening much longer, well, I just don't know. And my heart isn't good. I've got medicine from the doctor for my heart. And if you don't believe me you see Dr Forbes and check that. He'll tell you I'm not a well man. You phone him.'

'I'll be honest with you,' I started. 'If the Council and the police can't do anything about the boy in your roof, there's very little that I can do.'

'Can't you go up and interview him and tell him to go away?'

'If you're having trouble seeing him, he's not going to stay around for a stranger. Is there anyone else you can send up there?'

'We don't have too many friends now.'

'Look, I'm sorry. He probably wouldn't give me a story and could well get nasty with me. I really am sorry but I'm up to my nostrils in work. I've got to type out all the sides of Saturday's match. But I promise to pass all this on to Mr Hegarty when he gets back.'

'Who?'

'Mr Hegarty, the editor.'

'Why would you want to do that? You're not going to use our names are you? It'd kill the wife. She doesn't know I'm doing this. I had to wait until she went out for the messages before making this call. If you use our names, I'll get my lawyers on to you. I'm telling you . . .'

'Honestly, I don't know your name so I couldn't use it even if I wanted to. And as I said, there's little hope of us being able to do anything about this boy.'

'So you're not going to help us?'

'No, I'm afraid not.'

'So, I've been wasting my time?'

'The only thing I can suggest is that you get a friend to go up in your roof. After all, it might only be possums.'

'No – no, I don't think so,' he said. 'Possums wouldn't eat my wife's cooking.'

And it was finished. The budgie call of the week, of many weeks, was finally over. For the rest of the dying afternoon I did not type a word, but sat in my chair staring at the window and imagining the piles of rotting, mouldy food gathering dust in the roof of a house somewhere hereabouts. And the old, childless couple – if there ever was a wife – living with the sad conviction that there is a boy in their roof.

Father and Son

Far away from the clamour of warring nations, some way distant from the realms of government, and even beyond spitting distance of the Shire office, the town was a world of its own. Elsewhere revolutionaries overthrew corrupt juntas, scientists split atoms and actresses swallowed sleeping tablets. The other world was a groaning mass spinning on another orbit and watched from a distance. This world was different and watched from within.

Big cities were bad for the spirit, so consensus went. Other countries gave you stomach troubles, and you couldn't make yourself understood. There wasn't another place on earth so blessed and so beautiful as this one. Catch a local in a good mood and they'd swear to it on their mother's life. They spoke as if Paradise had always been here, hidden far away on the long plains, and would always remain so. Lesser men could only imagine; this mob was certain. All other towns, all other places, were ripe for contempt.

For Tingalla there was a special, keener distaste which sprung from the generation which first cut the roads across the plains to this place, which grubbed out the obstinate trees and planted fences and dreamed of a pub for the town.

For its football team, Tingalla had a side that had won the division premiership for years. They always beat our home team. Hands, feet and nostrils down and into the dust – their side was better.

Their crime was a cardinal one. They bought players. They paid sums that, when reported to strong men, made them stare stonily at the floor. For all the dedication to the sport in these parts, and it was a dedication sacerdotal passed through the milk of their mothers, there was never any money in it.

When Tingalla came to play at the home town oval, extra police were called in to handle the local crowd, who considered such action an insult and an obstruction. It was enough to make a few of them vow to stop paying their taxes. When our team played at Tingalla, few of their supporters considered it a match worthy of attendance. That enraged the visitors more than anything. They howled their rage across the oval at the empty stands and greeted the start of the game like wild creatures stung to blind frenzy. What usually followed was a game to take the wind out of our players and put it right up our supporters.

Among the most valiant of the defeated was always the Parker boy, who earned a large share of his praise by dint of his size and strength on the field. Accuracy and cunning were considerations not highly featured in a game where spectators wanted simple bloody revenge. Three months ago he had flattened Tingalla's star forward with a backhand swipe, and could still claim a free beer at Molloy's for it.

The Parker boy was old man Parker's eldest son, a lad equipped with shoulders worthy of the footballer he was. The shop packhorse, he could hoist fifty-pound sacks up and out of the shop with scarcely a grunt.

Parker's Food and Farm Goods Store was what could be called atmospheric. It was dark. It was old. And it would stay old until the last Parker died and a supermarket chain bought it and dragged it fighting into the present. Old man Parker had some links by marriage to the Tilsons. It was unlikely that the ancestral line would be broken for many years hence.

The story went that, when the 1933 bushfires licked right to the edge of Federation Street, someone grabbed the heavy metal till single-handed to save it from the flames. The shops were saved and the till was returned – empty. Even today the speculation about who made off with Parker's takings was lively, while the till itself sat prominent on the wide wooden counter of the store. Ornately embellished with swirls and cherubim, it received a weekly polish like the Holy of Holies, and rang out a lusty hymn in the archaic language of shillings and pence.

Cool and dark, with a polished wood floor, the shop was divided along its length, half for groceries, half for farm goods. Drenching kits nestled alongside 'Hats Brown and Black size seven', and there were packets of feed supplement and boxes of elastic braces, riding crops and big sacks of layer pellets stacked high against the far wall.

Old man Parker himself, a man whose massive girth had slipped in later years to settle around the waist, stood behind the till, directing the traffic of family staff and familiar customers with a wide, ruddy smile. He knew as much about anyone as anyone, and told as much as them all.

He didn't like me. He was the only man to tell me to my face that I was a blow-in. And he belonged to one of those new religions that barred him from entering Molloy's. The women seemed to like him.

Shopping at Parker's meant parading the intricacies of your domestic life. It was an ordeal for the impatient and the unprepared and went something like this.

'Morning.'

'Morning, dear.' He called every female customer 'dear', they seemed to like that. 'And how are we today?'

'Quite well, and yourself?'

'Oh yes, quite well, thank you. I only wish the weather would make up its mind.'

'Awful, isn't it.'

'Yes.'

'And how's Bob?'

'Very well. His lungs are better now. But he can't decide whether or not to sow now or perhaps wait a bit.'

'He's starting to leave it a bit late.'

'Yes. I told him so myself.'

And so the conversation would amble on for a while, comparing the doings of other farmers, the families of other farmers, and the health of everyone.

'I'd like peas please, Mr Parker.'

'Quite right. We can't spend all day standing here talking,' he'd say. 'Peas, you said, dear? Canned, dried or frozen?'

'Are the canned ones with mint?'

Mr Parker would rub his face slowly, turn to the wall of shelves packed tightly with groceries and wander its length several times, murmuring, 'Peas, peas. Now let's see if we have canned peas.' Then he would go and get the heavy wooden ladder, drag it to the shelf and set it stable. It was a slow process made slower by his bulk. Laboriously he would climb the ladder, reach for a can and examine its label over the top of his glasses.

'We have canned peas, dear. We have peas, processed with mint,' he would call down to the customer.

'Do you have any without mint?'

Mr Parker would then take a good long look along the shelves and say 'Can't see any up here. Hang on a second. We may have some out the back.'

Then he would carefully lower himself down the ladder, walk to the back store-room and emerge some while later saying, 'Sorry, dear. Haven't even got them out the back.'

'Then I'll just have to take the ones with the mint, although the boys don't like them much.'

'How many cans, dear?'

'Three, please.'

And he would slowly climb the ladder again.

'Three cans of peas – with mint,' he'd say, ringing up the price.

Every purchase by every customer, the pattern was unaltered. Shopping lists became public knowledge and the topic for dinner-table discussions around the town.

The arrival of the Parker boy one day in my office was a surprise. I hadn't considered him to be a reader of the *Weekly Advertiser*. I would have thought newspapers were, in his estimation, used only for wrapping groceries at his father's shop. He looked more sheepish than a runaway farmdog, and had a fat, black shiner where his left eye should have been. He shambled in, mumbled, took a seat and sniffed noisily. Eloquence comes hard for some people.

'You write the paper, don't you?' he started, giving me a sideways squint.

'Yes.'

'And you say what goes in and what doesn't?'

'To a point.'

'You wrote that piece on Mick Mollison dying?'

'Yes.'

'Yeh. Well... I'm here to give you something to put in that paper of yours. Something about my dad.'

'Mr Parker?'

'Yeh. Mr Parker.' He thrust his nose up in the air. There

was more than a hint of vinegar to this young Parker. 'Yes, Mr Godalmighty himself Parker. Someone should take him out and shoot him. Right mongrel he is.' Then followed a description of the dumpy shopkeeper that was colourful, if unprintable.

'Is he the one who landed you that punch?'

'Yeh. Can you believe it? And him the bloody church-goer and what have you. There he is on one hand preaching "good will" and "lay off the grog" and "Jesus Saves" and in the next minute he's beating up his own son when no one's looking.'

'I don't understand. What brought this on?' I asked.

'Buggered if I know.'

'Did you say something to him?'

'Not really.'

'What did you say?'

'I told him . . . I told him . . .' He spoke as if he had trouble with his adenoids. 'I told him that I wasn't gonna be working for him any more. That I wasn't gonna play footy for the team any more. I told him I was, I mean, I told him I was . . . moving out of town.'

'Where are you moving to?'

'Tingalla.'

'Why?'

'Looking for a proper job.'

'Are you going to play for Tingalla?'

'Yes.'

'Is that really why you're moving?'

'Yes.'

I stretched my legs under the desk. I stretched my back and shoulders and flexed each of my fingers. I once covered a yoga seminar.

'Is he the first person you've told?'

'My oath. And the only one – apart from you.'

'Why tell me?'

'It's just that I thought your piece on Jack Mollison was ace. I reckon you must be a good writer. I was never much one for English and all that, but I would've liked to do what you're doing. Anyway – it's too late now. I'm clearing out of town today. It's not worth my while hanging around this place – not when the news gets out. And I've just been packing and I was thinking how much I wanted to get that bastard once and for all before I go. Before I leave I want to give him this.' He raised a one-fingered salute. 'Here's to you – Mr Parker. And I was hoping you'd put something in the paper to expose him for the bastard he is.'

It must have been the longest speech in his life. I had to think hard before I answered.

'He's going to miss you in the shop.'

'Bugger his bloody shop.'

'You probably would have inherited it.'

'Couldn't give his shop a stuff. I really couldn't. It and he can take a long, running jump for all I care. I don't want his bloody shop. I'll get this money and set myself up in Tingalla. Might get some trucking work.'

'How much have they offered you for the team transfer?'

'Enough.'

'How much is enough?'

'Enough for . . . for what I need it for.'

'What do you need it for?'

'Things. Just things. Food, clothes, I guess. Stuff like that.'

'I think you need it for something in particular. What else?'

'Nothing.' His reply was sharp and I let a silence between us say more. 'It's just that I need this money real quick,' he said.

'What for?'

'To pay . . . to pay for . . .'

'Bets?'

'No.'

'Drugs?'

'Oh no. No. Nothing like that. To pay a doctor. A doctor down in Melbourne. My girlfriend . . .'

'Forgot?'

'I suppose so.'

'Or you did?'

'I dunno.'

'Couldn't your dad lend you the money?'

'Fair suck! Not in a million years. And if he found out what I needed it for. If he knew that Charlene was . . . was, you know . . . Hell, he'd run me out of town.'

'But he's running you out of town as it is,' I said.

'Yeh, I know. But it's different.'

'Why haven't you already taken heel and run?'

He shrugged. 'Don't know, really. Didn't seem the right thing.'

'Seems to me you must have some time for this girl.'

'Yeh well . . . I suppose so. Yeh, reckon I must.'

'And what does she think about all this?'

'Doesn't like the idea much. But there's nothing else we can do.'

'You certain?'

'Christ! I've tried to think of everything.'

'You know it'll not only mean you losing your family. There's her family too. They're bound to turn against her.'

'Yeh, yeh, I know. We both know.'

'And you wouldn't think of getting married?'

'Oh no. No. People in this town may be a bit thick, but they can count backwards.'

'Seems to me they've had plenty of experience. You know, these kinds of weddings aren't all that unusual in this town. Anyway, who's to say you've got to get married here?'

'Where else is there?'

'Where are you going?'

The thick, unbroken line of his eyebrows rose and slid back into his chair. 'Tingalla,' he said.

'Tingalla,' I said. 'And what are you planning to do with that transfer fee?'

'Like I said, we'll go to Melbourne and . . .'

'And pay it to some doctor who needs the money far less than you do. You sound like you could do with that money, especially if you were to get married and have a wife . . .'

'And a kid.' You could almost hear his brain cells scraping together.

'But you'll need a lot of money to get started. And someone with a lot of money is your dad.'

'Nah. Not a hope.'

'How would you know? He might be pleased to know that his son's settling down with a wife and family. He'd certainly be pleased to tell people that.'

'Maybe. I don't know.'

'You won't know if he doesn't know. And he won't know until you tell him.'

'I gotta think on this one.'

'And I've got to go and do an interview. I'm already running late. You can stay here if you want to have a think. No one comes in here this time of the day.'

'Ta. Yeh, thanks. I will.'

I took a long drive out past the lake, choosing a road that skirted the edge of the red country and one much favoured by motorists aware that the police never used it for speed-traps. On the slow return journey I counted four dead wallabies and at least a dozen dead birds by the roadside. The road sign warning 'Kangaroos – Next 50 km.' had been used by carloads of youths for target practice. It was now a flat metal sieve, shot through with ·22 pellets. If it moves, shoot it. If it doesn't, ditto.

He was still there when I returned, head bowed.

'Still thinking?' I asked.

'Christ! No.' His voice seemed to explode from his chest. 'I finished thinking. I did something for a change.'

'What's that?'

'Guess.'

'You went to see your dad.'

'Right in one.'

'And he agreed to give you some money.'

'Not only that,' he said. 'Not only that.' He looked up. A new black swelling was already starting to bloom over his right eye. 'And he reckons he'll buy you a drink at the wedding,' he said with a smile like a mile length of picket fence.

A Fist of Fives

Hegarty was riled.

The editor was angry, and the heavens, or more probably the depths, knew no such fury. I heard it all as I pushed open the door to the press-room.

'You low, scheming little quisling,' Hegarty's voice yelled from his office. 'You're an insult to humanity. A parasite. A blood-sucker. A mean little money-grabber.'

The rest of the staff sat back in pleasure. They followed the tirade of insults with mock grimaces as each salvo was launched from the open door.

'You're a bloody leech that stains the name of all bookmakers everywhere.'

His insults were obviously directed at Pat. The door to the camera-room was closed.

'You're the low sort of mongrel that spits on the sport of kings. Lower than a worm's codpiece, you are.'

Having run the gamut of his vocabulary, Hegarty now took a pause, and in the ceasefire a few of the printers slid off quickly to the toilet and returned just as quickly, fearing they might miss more of the entertainment.

'You know I could sack you if I wanted to,' bellowed Hegarty. He was right, too.

'And you'd never get a better bromide operator. Not on these wages,' yelled back Pat. He was right, too.

Throughout the press-room all activity had stopped. The presses were ignored. The usual jangle of noise and motion from the linotype was stilled. There was no flurry of newsprint curled up and crumpled into the corners by the scuff of feet. As a press-room it had always seemed frozen in time and now it seemed frozen for all time. The printers ranged around the room silently, masking their smirks with their huge, inky hands. A printer never has clean hands. The ink of years lodges fast into every pore, every whorl of the skin, and never leaves. If there is a Heaven for printers, and if any of them ever qualify for entry, it shall always have fingerprints on the doorhandle.

Hegarty exploded through his door and screamed across the room. 'You just come in here and step into my office.'

The printers scattered like guilty cats, scurrying to their posts in an effort to look busy. Blind to everything but his anger, Hegarty ignored them.

'Did you hear me?' he roared.

'Yes,' said Pat, appearing at his door, rubbing his hands leisurely on a cloth but reddening violently around the neck. Squatter and more solid than his boss, he had a lower centre of gravity and was not easily overturned. He finished wiping his hands, he closed his door and walked the length of the press-room to vanish behind the slammed door of the editor's office.

'Right,' Hegarty's voice started, and then sank into a murmur.

'Do you reckon something's happening in there?' I whispered aside to Martha.

She dropped her smile into a decorous grin and motioned me out to her front reception desk in the corridor.

'Nothing to do with horses, I suppose?' I asked.

'No, no,' said Martha, setting about the business of tidying up last week's return of papers. 'Nothing at all,' she said, straightening the pages and stacking the bundles against the wall. And smiling.

'And I don't suppose it has anything to do with horses running at Melbourne last Saturday?'

'Of course not,' said Martha, still smiling as she frowned at the ink on her hands.

'And I would probably be wrong in assuming that someone in this office put some money on at least one of those horses?'

'Probably.'

'Money invested on the advice of another staff member known to have an interest in such things?'

'Hmm?' said Martha as she sorted through her advertising receipts.

'A staff member known to have a financial interest in such

things? Otherwise known as a bookmaker? A starting price bookmaker – perhaps?'

'Perhaps.'

'Go on, Martha. Tell me. What odds did Pat snaffle him for?'

Martha looked at me blandly. 'Odds? Odds? Are they those twenty-five to one sort of things?'

From all her years of employment at the *Weekly Advertiser*, Martha had come to know about diplomacy. For all his years of employing Pat, Hegarty had never learned that a bookmaker likes to make money. And so he might rail and flap his arms, for Pat, with all the knowledge about everything that he had, knew just how to make the monkey dance.

They were at it a very long time. Their voices swelled all the while as Hegarty accused Pat of grand deception and Pat demanded payment. They were at it like a pair of tropical fighting fish.

Suddenly there was a thud of flesh on flesh and Pat lunged out, holding his head. He rushed to the camera-room and slammed the door. There was silence around the print-room and, in that silence, a new respect for the editor.

I left what I thought was a reasonable delay before tapping at the door. 'Pat? Pat? Are you all right in there?'

'Come in, come in. Quickly. Close the door after you.'

Pat had a telephone receiver in one hand and with the other waved me into a chair. He was discussing odds and figures of money that ranged high into four figures. He seemed agitated and swivelled around on his seat. When he put the receivers down, they slammed, and he grabbed one up again with impatience as he dialled another number. There followed a succession of calls made in this way and then a string of calls coming in. When at last he had finished his business, he turned to me, flushed and fierce-looking.

'What a man must do for a living, eh? Makes you weep tears of blood,' he said.

'If I could understand what's going on – I would,' I said.

'It's a bookie's nightmare for next Saturday. None of the favourites is up to form and the stayers aren't up to much either. The fields are all over the place like a tart's favours.' He took a breath. 'The lads in town are running around like headless chooks and the odds are up and down like a wedding night.'

I could only nod in mock comprehension. The world of race-going and the mechanics of this slightly illegal style of betting forever challenged my understanding.

'I nearly lost out wasting time in that little discussion with Hegarty,' he continued, reaching under his chair for a reviver. The bottle was nearly empty.

'You both seemed engrossed,' I offered, feigning a casual air. 'What was it all about?'

'You wouldn't want to know.'

'I guess not,' I said, and was rewarded with an offer of the bottle. Pat gave a soft laugh as I returned it. 'Ah . . . stupid old so-and-so.'

'Hegarty?'

'No.' He chuckled some more. 'Although, I must say, his timing was not ideal. He might have waited until I'd finished my phone-calls.'

'Did he hurt you?'

'Who?'

'Hegarty.'

'When?'

'When he hit you.'

Pat seemed to smile to himself. 'No, no,' he mumbled. 'Not at all. Positively therapeutic,' he added. He took a long, ruminating draw of the bottle and muttered enigmatically, 'Pride. There's a lot of it about.'

'But did you get your money?'

'There are some things *even* beyond the price of Mammon,' he said, nursing the bottle in his palms. 'There is reputation and respect. Francis Hegarty had to prove he wasn't going to take defeat. So we came to a . . . an agreement.'

He watched my bewilderment with delight, and then, slowly putting his bottle down, he lifted both his hands up. With a loud report, he slapped the fist of one into the palm of the other, then grabbed at his face and reeled backwards. And then he smiled and gave me a wink.

'You see, a man needs a very good excuse not to honour his racing debts,' he said.

'Hegarty owes you?'

'Let's just say he was contemplating payment in kind.' He

lifted the receiver of one of the phones. 'These things do cost a lot to run, don't they.'

'But you let him hit you – or pretend to. Where's your reputation after that? Where's your respect?'

'I've yet to meet a dollar note I didn't like,' said Pat.

A Likely Contender

It was an unassailable right, a fact and a fortress sure, that no one contested local Council elections in these parts.

Councillors were elected unopposed to fill the posts left vacant by newly dead councillors. They served out their years, taking turns at the mayoralty until they died and the cycle continued. There was a tradition of father and son in some of the families, and at Cooree an aberration of father and daughter. But overall the basic rule remained as unshakeable as redgum posts.

To the practical country mind it meant a saving of needless election costs. To the more pessimistic it really didn't matter much anyway – a silly bunch of galahs such as councillors were.

'Those daft coots in the city can piddle around with campaigns,' said old man Tilson, dropping a butt half smoked into the bar trough. 'A man's got more to do than wimp and whelp for a scoungy vote or two.'

He had served four times as mayor and was awaiting his turn again two years hence, when his meaty style of local government would again assault the boundaries of traditional democracy. Elected to replace his father several decades before I was born, old man Tilson believed in straight-talking, the power of a clenched fist and the supreme right of a man to do what he wanted – particularly if it was for profit. A supremely successful businessman, and one admired, if not really liked, by most, his opinions were forged steel-hard and known by all. He could whip up into a fine rage when he felt it necessary, and for that reason was known around the office of the *Weekly Advertiser* as 'Dial-a-Quote Tilson'. Hegarty considered himself a wise man to keep the councillor as a friend.

Tilson's son, a man of a more moderate disposition, figured that a serious angina was the only barrier between him and control of Tilson's Reliable Garage and his father's Council seat. And for that he was patiently waiting his time.

The chance of a heart-attack striking the old man down was perilously close that warm afternoon in the shelter of Molloy's marvellous hostelry. The old fellow was holding angry and vehement audience among the lunch-time drinkers, having just heard news from the Shire Secretary that someone had lodged their application to contest his seat in the next local election. Old man Tilson vowed by Hell that he'd beat this opponent, this mongrel scum, this out-and-out bastard and right bugger. The air in the pub was thickening with each curse, and finally Mick Molloy told him to turn it down a bit because the noise was carrying through to the ladies' lounge.

A great deal of Tilson's rage came from his frustration in not knowing the identity of his challenger. The form posted to the Shire office at Nooweep had said only D. R. Westgrove – a surname that not even old man Tilson could recognise. He foamed in fury, testing the memories of everyone in Molloy's as to who it could be.

By leaving the front bar, walking past the butcher's and the Kookaburra Café and then into my office at the *Weekly Advertiser*, he could have known. The contender that had been sitting there awaiting my return from lunch. She rose from the chair as I walked into my office. Pulling back a strand of long hair, she came up and offered a handshake. She was holding a wad of papers.

'Hello,' she said. 'I'm Dianne Westgrove.'

I confess my attention rested less on the greeting than on the small child burrowing through the piles of papers on my desk. A boy, I presumed, although it was difficult to be precise, and of an age that was worrisome.

'Vivian, come to Mummy.' She had seen my anxiety.

'Have a seat, Don't worry about him. We get all kinds in here.' I blushed at the gaffe, and tried to restart the conversation as I gathered the papers scattered by the small hands. 'You're standing for Council, I hear.'

'Yes.'

'Against old man Tilson.'

'Who? Yes, I suppose so. I'm not too familiar with some of

the councillors,' she said. 'I try to keep personalities out of politics.'

'You're not from around here?'

'I'm living out at Michaelson's corner.'

'But you're not from here?'

'Not exactly. I've come up from Melbourne, although my parents lived at Tingalla for a time, when I was small.'

Already images were dashing into the mud of my mind. A female standing for Council, a female from the city. If those odds weren't bad enough, a female with a childhood in this town's arch sporting rival . . . Old man Tilson had more ammunition than he knew. Than she knew.

'And so I thought that, since I am relatively unknown here, I should drop in and introduce myself, and' – she passed over her wad of papers – 'perhaps suggest an article for the paper.'

I cast an eye over the sheets, and it bounced over several very thick paragraphs about local consultation at local government level. The page was jammed tight with grey type. I could only manage to plough through the first few paragraphs before saying, 'First, let's get some details about you.'

'What sort?' She did not seem comfortable.

'How long have you been here?' I began.

'About eight months. I know it's not long but I'm used to settling into an area quickly. I'm quite adaptable.'

'How's that? You've shifted a lot, I take it?'

'Well, yes, I have. More than I'd like to make too public.' She was teetering along a thread of indecision. 'I've had to move for personal reasons. I'm separated from my husband. Do I have to tell you any more?'

'If you want to. That side of things is not too important to the story,' I said, laying down my pen.

Her story was rambling. Her speech was not: clipped and bitter evidence of the cruelty that only men and women can inflict on each other. She told me more than I expected and more than she had intended.

'And so I decided to get out of the city and away into the country. I lodged a request with the Education Department and they posted me as an emergency teacher for this region. The work hasn't been thick on the ground, but it does,' she said.

'But why stand for Council?'

She waved at the papers I held. 'I believe local government, more than any other sphere of government, has a responsibility of directness to its community – the community which elected it and the community as a whole. I used to study politics. Local government must be responsible but it also needs to be responsive. It must...'

'...You right bugger. You little shit. What the hell did you mean by writing...?' Hegarty exploded into the room. 'Oh I'm sorry.' He did not sound at all apologetic.

'I've got some shopping to do. Come on, Vivian.' She dashed for the door, and I could not decide if it was tact or terror that spurred her flight.

Hegarty didn't draw a breath. 'You bastard – what do you think you were doing?'

The folds of skin around his throat were flapping wildly. The long and bony lengths of his arms were dashing at the air. He looked like an aged and scrawny crow struggling with lift-off.

'What's up?' I asked. 'What's wrong?'

His voice dropped dangerously quiet. 'What did you write in that editorial last week?' His voice jumped several decibels. 'And why the hell haven't I read it?'

I must have gaped. He jumped into the gap. 'That bloody editorial.' He stalked the room, turning angrily on his heels. 'How the hell was I to know? Gave the cops a grand old laugh. Bloody laughing at me. As if a man can't have a drink.'

I recalled the piece I'd done on drunken driving. 'Well, it came out of that Mollison accident. The one where Jack Mollison died and the kid in hospital and all,' I said.

He spun around. 'I couldn't give a flea's arsehole about Mick Mollison – nor the kid. Just what did you say?'

'I suggested that with so many police concentrated in the south of the district and around Nooweep, it might be wise to post a few more up here to stop accidents like Mollison's.'

'Anything else?'

'Well –' I shuffled some papers across my desk. 'I might have had a bit of a sling-off, saying the cops should pull up their socks a bit. It was the third accident in as many months. And it seemed that...'

'It seemed that. It *seemed*.' Hegarty's voice was now just below the threshold of pain. 'A bit of a sling-off?' He paced the floor, two steps in each direction, fuming. 'All right, you slime, listen to this,' he said. 'Last night I had a couple of beers and I got into my car and I drove home, and just before I got there I was stopped for a breath test by some pimply-faced turd in a blue uniform. And do you know where he was? He was waiting for me right outside my driveway – right outside my home. He was waiting for me.'

'Well . . .'

'Now don't you give me your moralising and don't you go apologising either. I'm angry and I want to be angry. I'd like to be angrier, if it were possible. You are stupid. You are very stupid. You haven't got two brain cells to rub together. You idiot. You idiotic . . . idiot.'

He started into coughing fits from the exertion of it all. I handed him the remains of my coffee. He stood a long time drawing in deep breaths. 'Agh, shit it,' he mumbled, and turned out of the room.

A few days later I found his note on my desk. From now on, it said, he would want to see all the editorials before publication. And would I be kind enough to be a character witness at his court hearing?

Power to the People

The sound of hammering coming from inside the Kookaburra Café was patchy. It set off in a burst and faded into sporadic strokes. It had started early on Thursday morning and stopped for a long time during lunch. It had the regulars of Molloy's puzzled.

Parked outside the building was a ute of unknown vintage and ownership. Passers-by would stop to inspect it, but could remember no owner of such a pitiful piece of machinery. They were likewise mystified about the intermittent sounds of renovation from within the building. They stood there on the footpath trying to see between the sheets of paper pasted up on the windows, and then moved on quickly when they realised others were watching.

Public interest in this building was deep-centred. The last owners were a Greek family who stayed only a short while before disappearing back to the city under a certain persuasion brought on by the nocturnal activities of the elder son with a local girl. During their time they made few friends, and it was said their pies were served many days old. More ancient locals were always suspicious of café food, considering it nutritionally inferior to home-cooked fare. Their young would not have made that distinction and would have looked to the café as an established meeting place and eatery. But the word got around that you'd have to be desperate to eat there, and few were that desperate. In the end everyone avoided the place, having exchanged dire tales of what had been seen going into the kitchen at the back. Not having been in town at the time, I could not swear to the stories, but they were told with such regularity and conviction that it may have been true that stray cats, minced offal and foul-smelling vats from the Nooweep knackery had been served up.

'And it was always so dirty,' Martha whispered in her knowing, conspiratorial way. 'Never swept the floors, much less polished. Never any tablecloths or anything. Filthy.'

The crowd at Molloy's, eager to know what was going on behind the paper screen, pressed me into action.

'You're a reporter, you can go in there,' said one of the Printz boys, as if a pen and notepad guaranteed immunity from hepatitis and cholera. 'You can ask questions.'

'Find out who owns the pick-up. I need a side-door panel.'

'And ask them about the set of drill bits that never seems to get used. They'll just rust left in the open like that.'

My knock at the door was answered by a long stretch of blue denim I swear rose as high as my chest. Above it hung a checked shirt and, above that, a cascade of light brown beard that gleamed a most odd russet colour in the light.

'Good afternoon,' I started, explaining that I was the local reporter, that I worked next door, perhaps this was a story, perhaps I was just curious...

'Come in,' said a voice that dangled disconcertingly in the falsetto range. 'Pardon the mess.'

Expecting grease-spattered walls and black-slathered linoleum, I walked into a room of soft pine and suffused light. The sharp, sweet smell of fresh sawdust made the air fragrant. I have always found that smell one of the finest in life and have often thought carpenters to be sensualists at heart.

'You've done a lot of work in here,' I said.

'Not really. Hardly any.'

His hands were huge, ribbed with veins and bones and spread massively over his kneecaps as he folded himself into a chair. Mick Mollison had been big and strong. This fellow was tall and big and strong, but his face was pinched surprisingly thin and its skin pitted by some aberration of childhood hormones. Perhaps it was smallpox. Most of it was covered by the beard. Sheltered behind the same russet-coloured eyebrows were eyes of a resolute blackness. They could not even be called dark brown.

I could not start to guess his genetic inheritance.

His name was Nigs, he said. It was really Walter, but he insisted on the nickname. He pulled out a worn leather pouch and started the slow business of rolling a cigarette with those great hams of hands. He rolled it thin and tight and slow to burn.

'So, the local paper.' His voice was really most confusing, equipped as he was with such an ample sound-box of a chest. 'Like working here?'

'Better than not working anywhere.'

He almost smiled, I think. 'Tough living around here without a job.'

I couldn't figure if that was a question or a statement. 'Yes, but I'm a Melbourne exile.'

'How long have you been here then?'

'Almost ten months, I suppose.'

'You like this town?'

'They haven't drummed me out of here yet.'

'What's the paper like? Any good?'

'In parts. They treat me well. The editor stays in the shadows most of the time, so I'm my own one-man band.'

'You write most of the stuff that goes in?'

'Most, yes, I suppose so. Council, sport, police, hospital bazaars, the CWA – nothing to shake the foundations of the world of journalism.'

'Do you mind if I work while we talk?'

I had no objection, and watched, oddly enthralled, as he lifted the length of his body out of the chair. He moved around the scattered debris of timber off-cuts and tools like an elephant through a carpet of egg-shells. He was a tug-o'-war team in one set of muscles and the litheness of a schoolgirl in the other. I was fascinated by him more than one man should be by another.

Muscles flexing, he bent down smoothly and lifted a plank with one hand. I couldn't have done it with two.

'So, what are you planning to do here?' I asked.

'Are we on the record?'

'Yes.' It was a question I was asked rarely around here.

'Are you using a tape-recorder?'

'Come on – the *Weekly Advertiser* has only just got rid of its carrier pigeons and cleft sticks,' I said. 'Just a notebook and pen.'

He began with a long intake of breath. 'I am undertaking a conversation, not only of this building but of the entire capitalist system. I intend to draw upon traditional rural traditions of commerce – principally barter – in a co-operative attack against laissez-faire economies,' he said, measuring and marking a length of timber. 'Got that?'

He continued working. 'Traditional community-based enterprises have fallen pray to the vested interests and monetary policies of governments overruled by multi-national corporations, and I intend to prove to this town that grass-roots revolt will work.' He reached for another length of timber. 'How does that sound?'

I could only nod.

'There are more and more examples of people undertaking socialist ideals of communal ownership, communal operations and communal profit-sharing, and I believe it's time that this town joined that push.'

'Uh-huh,' I said, scribbling down the last of his words. 'But . . . er . . . but what are you going to do with the shop?'

'What do you mean?'

'What's it going to be?'

'A wholefoods co-operative.'

'What do you mean? Lentils and soya beans?'

'And hand-milled flours, bulk molasses, honeys. I'm hoping to persuade some of the farmers to grow organic fruit and vegetables for sale,' he said, in a shower of sawdust. 'People regaining control of food supply from the monopolies. And a restaurant, a small restaurant, offering the socialist alternative at fair prices so that there's just enough income to cover costs and provide a small dividend to shareholders. That's an important part of the project – communal ownership and operation between a wide range of people to prevent centralisation of power and wealth.'

'Have you got many shareholders?'

'Getting there,' he said, reaching for another piece of timber. 'And we could expand into other operations – a bookshop offering an alternative range of literature explaining socialist doctrines. Perhaps an art gallery too.'

'So it's a grocery-cum-café and possibly a bookshop and art gallery.' I chewed the end of my pen. 'But are you sure this the right place? Voters around here have never returned anyone to power but conservative politicians, and I doubt many of them would have been inside an art gallery in their lives.'

'All the more reason why a venture like this is needed in towns like this,' he said.

'What are you going to call it?'

'Engels. It seemed apt.'

'I think the meaning might be lost on some of the readers. Couldn't you just call it the Kookaburra Café?'

'We are talking social revolution here.'

'I see.'

'Strength through solidarity.'

I could see that the town's newly and self-appointed socialist conscience had set himself quite a task. In the words of Pat, when I told him the news: 'He's chosen a hard road for a small dog with a big dick.'

Public reaction to the news of the Engels Wholefood Community Co-operative Limited ranged from the incredulous to the unbelieving. I was branded a liar and a leg-puller for having put the words of Nigs into print.

'I don't know what he's on about,' said Mick Molloy.

'What on earth got into the Shire Council to give planning permission to a crank like that?' said Morrie.

'He didn't need planning permission. The building was already listed as a food store,' said old man Tilson.

'You standing up for him or something?' said Pete Maguire.

'Not in the least,' said Tilson. 'The last thing we need around this place is a bloody Commo.'

'He really hasn't done anything yet,' I said.

'It's what he is, not what he's done,' said Pete. 'He's a socialist. He said so himself. It was in the paper.'

'Can't believe everything you read in the paper,' said Pam, refilling my glass with a sly wink.

'Well, he did say he was a socialist,' I said.

'There you go,' said Tilson. 'I rest my case. The last thing we need in this town are people of communistic tendencies. Red-raggers supporting the unions. Teachers, a lot of them are teachers, you know. They're a disease. They really are. He'll be talking to the schoolkids next, infecting their minds with all his claptrap. And the next thing you know they'll all want to go to university and that's the start of the end. Dope-smoking, long-haired layabouts. They'll bring on revolution – that's what they're after, you know. Anarchy and bloodshed.'

'So far he's only said he wants to set up a grocery store,' I said.

'But that's just the start,' said Morrie. 'At first it's innocent-like. And suddenly, it isn't.'

'Anyway, how could you call that a grocery? Why do we need a shop like that?' said Tilson. 'Sunflower seeds and peanuts? Parrot food! Organic food? Like hell! I'd rather eat a bowl of bat-shit . . . wouldn't taste much different.'

'I bet he's one of those vegetarian types,' said Morrie. 'I bet he doesn't drink tea or coffee. I bet he uses dental floss.'

'He's probably into one of those weird Eastern religions, shaving his head or something.'

'He seemed to have a lot of hair,' I said.

'Ah, but they wear wigs.'

'And take drugs.'

'Bah,' said Pete. 'He should have stayed in the city. That's where he deserves to be.'

'And you can't tell me he's not going to make money out of this if he can help it,' said Tilson. 'Non-profit? It's not natural. And he's after shareholders? He'll be lucky to have people walk on the same side of the street as him, much less put their money into his harebrained scheme.'

'All this socialist talk – I reckon he's only in it for the quick buck,' said Morrie. 'I bet he's a closet capitalist. He's as bad as the rest.'

The agent of the Devil was measuring up curtains for the shop window when I called in. Green checked curtains with lace and frills at the bottom. His reaction to the story wasn't overwhelming either.

'Socialism is a moral philosophy as well as an economic one, and not to mention a proper noun. It's always spelled with a capital "s". Everyone knows that,' he said.

I took a seat, and watched while he pestered around trying to straighten the hem and then gave up the task altogether.

'Non-sexist labour is all very well,' he said, sinking his massive frame to the floor and pulling out the ingredients for another of his thin cigarettes. 'But I've still got to finish writing my treatise on Leninist ideology as it applies to rural working classes.' He was thinking aloud. 'Perhaps I could get some unemployed girl – I mean unemployed person – to do this work.

I could offer them the work in exchange for shares in the co-operative.'

'How are the shares selling?' I asked.

'Fine, fine,' he said, bringing a match up to the cigarette. He inhaled and released a cloud, watching it drift away. 'Slowly.'

'Do you mean badly?'

'Maybe. But once the place is opened and people see it is a viable enterprise, then it'll really pick up,' he said.

'Really?'

'Oh yes.'

'But can you carry it financially until then?'

'I think so. I've applied for some government grants and I'm hoping the Council will chip in a bit, as an employment project.'

None of this sounded hopeful and I changed the subject.

'When are you planning to open for business?'

'Well, there's a few problems come up. Getting supplies and things like that.' He wandered across to the other side of the room. 'I had hoped to open this month, but now it looks like next.'

'No one said the transformation of Western society would be easy.'

'No,' he said, looking out of the window and stroking his beard.

'And in the meantime?'

'I'll be working here and trying to attract shareholders.' He turned suddenly. 'That reminds me. I tell you who has shown some interest – that woman standing for the Shire Council.'

'Dianne Westgrove?'

'Yes, yes, her. Said that if she was elected she'd push for Council funding for this place. She dropped in yesterday and spent a long while here. I told her all about it and she seemed to take to the idea. She said someone should make a documentary about the formation of a co-operative in a small country town. Really good idea. Progressive. And I suggested some of the kids from her school might like to make it. They've got video cameras. Or we could even set up a communications workshop here. Once the restaurant's off the ground we could also have a side-line with a community video co-operative. And we could sell the documentary to the capital city television stations. She said she'd look into it for me. Smart woman, that one.'

83

'A film?'

'Yeh. A documentary concentrating on real social needs. A sort of explanation of socialist doctrine in practical terms. A type of counterpoint to ingrained rural conservatism, a struggle against economics imposed from above by capitalist monopolies...'

As I listened I wrestled hard with the feeling that someone, somewhere, had a lot to answer for.

A Family Wedding

It had been a quiet wedding. The church pews were scattered with only a handful of people. Their voices were thin and self-conscious as they laboured through the hymns. The poor attendance was unusual in this part of the world, where news of a wedding usually brought all the women into town to stand outside the church and wait for a glimpse of the bride and her dress. They were the sort of women who dressed bride dolls, which were then raffled to other women who would place them in the middle of their beds as daytime decoration. And they were the type of women who would spend hours with icing sugar and pipettes practising elaborate decoration of bells and doves on blocks of wood. Or the sort who would crochet bridal dresses for small dolls which were then used to cover over and hide rolls of toilet paper or milk jugs. It all seemed a most peculiar fixation, and not necessarily a healthy one.

But Tingalla was a long way distant from the town and the Parker family had kept news of their son's impending marriage very quiet. My invitation had been penned, pushed into an envelope and quickly shoved into my hand as an unspoken pact to secrecy. Come the appointed day, I put on my suit, drove to Tingalla and joined the few trusted souls allowed to witness the marriage of the broad-shouldered boy to his quick-swelling girlfriend. Twins, at least.

The old wooden church stood far out into the bush north of the town. The tussocks of sedge and long grass seemed never to have seen the business end of a mower, and brushed against the thighs of the guests filing out of the church. Old man Parker slipped away from the rest of the group to visit the little leaning toilet, standing like a forgotten sentrybox way across the paddock. He returned looking white. 'Bloody black snake curled up behind the door,' he whispered as he took up his position with the rest of the bridal party.

Someone threw confetti. No one took photographs. Smiles for the most part were fixed tight as the vicar tried to lighten the mood with a string of mild-mannered jests. Eventually even he sensed the atmosphere, looked around uncertainly and quickly took his leave. He locked the church, got into his car and drove back along the thin, winding track back into town.

Looking befuddled as a flock of lost sheep, the group of guests hung back at the church door. The women in gloves and wide-brimmed hats, the men in dark suits, the children scrubbed and polished and forced into best clothes – all stood around chatting politely and waving away the flies. Heavy-bodied black bushflies they were, hanging lazily in the air. The drone of their flight merged with the thick sound of the crickets' chirrups. The bride's mother spent most of her time and concentration swiping them off the back of her daughter's gown. The look on her face was one of ill-disguised loathing.

The group filtered into cars and the cars headed away in dust and noise to the small hall hidden yet further in the bush. It was built of wood and iron and would have looked less dowdy had it not been painted, many years ago, in panels of different colours obviously offered in one cheap job-lot. At the rear of the room were trestle tables set up with food. The lines of bottles offered refreshments more innocent than is normally seen at wedding receptions. It was obvious that the Parker family practised what their patriarch preached.

Across the floor was strewn a thick layer of sawdust. The boards beneath were polished slippery smooth. The children quickly sensed the game in it and skidded with laughter along the length of the hall, carefully ignoring the admonitions of their parents as they did so.

There was a cluster of men around the drinks table, and those women not fussing around the plates of food were standing around the pile of wedding presents opened and displayed for public inspection. The food served out on paper plates was typical buffet fare of cold, sliced meats and salad, presenting everyone with the everlasting problem of balancing a drink and a plate, spearing food and managing to eat it standing up without causing social disgrace. The few chairs along the far wall were reserved for the infirm. The old people sat, legs spread and shoulders hunched over their plates, chewing their food silently and delicately, maintaining, even with plastic cutlery and fragile plate, a dining decorum lost to more recent generations. The children who flocked to the table at first had now eaten their fill. A young girl with long sausage-curls in her vivid orange hair was now engaged in biting her slice of ham into a lace doily pattern. The boy beside her was trying tomato ketchup with everything. The rest of their plates were abandoned half-picked as they ran outside. A toddler sat beside its mother, pushing a piece of bread through the sawdust and gumming on it distractedly. Pregnant women – and there seemed to be a number of them – shook their heads as more food was heaped on to their plates. Other women who looked pregnant were doing the same. Pride and tradition demand that no one goes hungry in this part of the world.

Reigning magnificent in the centre of the table was the cake, a baroque creation of many tiers held apart with plastic fluted columns and sitting on a platter wrapped in silver paper. The labour of many hours, it was covered with flat white icing and wreathed in sugar flowers and ribbons. Finely piped lace trickled across the top and cascaded down the sides. The sight of it stirred murmurs from the crowd, and they launched into a cheer when the newly-weds cut into it. The smile on the face of the Parker boy was a nervous one, the expression of a man unused to bow tie and hired suit. Beside him, Charlene undertook alternating bouts of blushing and giggling. She bit her bottom lip. She covered her mouth. She uncovered her mouth and bit the top of her finger. She picked at a piece of thread on her sleeve. She brushed some crumbs from the front of her gown and smiled. She twisted a strand of hair around her finger. She waved to some friends.

'If I could please have your attention a moment...' old man Parker called out. 'Please, just a minute. We've got a bit of a programme here and a few speeches to get through.' He paused to cast an eye down to the book he held. *Bridal Etiquette*, the cover said. 'First of all, I'll ask the best man to read out the telegrams.' His wife tugged at his elbow and whispered something to him, I supposed as a reminder that whoever was supposed to know about the wedding was in the hall. 'Ah, yes,' the father said. 'So now we move along to' – he stopped a moment to consult his guide – 'the speech by the bride's father.'

Laconic these people were, and their speech-making was rudimentary. Thanks were extended and best wishes expressed while the guests stood around, shuffling their feet slowly through the sawdust. Their applause was more polite than heart-felt. Like the speeches, it was part of the formalities and a requirement for such an occasion.

Tom Sayers and the Metrotones were a hardy annual for this kind of function. Each of the three musicians had celebrated more than fifty years on stages of small halls like this around the district. In that time they had never changed their style nor their repertoire, and for that were evergreen favourites. There was applause as Tom took his time-worn seat behind his drums. Mrs Sayers smiled and waved before sitting at the old upright piano, while her brother Geoffrey finished dusting the rosin off his violin. There was a hush as the musicians tuned up and, with a quiet 'one, two, three' from Tom, the music started.

They launched into 'Shuffling off to Buffalo' as if they'd just discovered Christmas. So often had they performed this opener that they did not have to concentrate on the music they produced. It simply pealed out of their instruments as they set to enjoying themselves, all foot-tapping and broad smiles and singing as if they had done nothing else since birth. Tom held the rhythm tight but unhurried. He played drums as a man of his age should, letting the whirr of the brushes against the drum fill in the moments when the melody paused. Mrs Sayer had the technique of a pianist accustomed to large halls. Dexterity was a poorer cousin to volume in her hands, and she thumped through the bass chord progressions with a familiar ease. She made me think of a wartime trooper charged with the task of jollying the front-line soldiers. It remained to Geoffrey to claim the melody line, and this he clearly enjoyed as he stood there sawing away gaily at the strings and weaving his body to the tempo. There was not a soloist among them but they were never the poorer for that. They pushed out the finale with gusto and barely stopped to acknowledge the applause, for theirs was the task of keeping up the music and getting the guests up and on to the dance floor.

It did not take long. The women stood down one side of the hall, the men down the other, but slowly a few husbands drifted over to claim their partners for the quickstep. Like the leaders of an ant swarm, they were soon followed by the rest. The mood spread outwards from the stage and into the rest of the hall. Soon the floor was bouncing with a lively mixture of conversation and moving bodies.

Men nodded to each other as they passed and women leaned over their shoulders to catch at conversations floating by. Heels kicked higher and a few couples launched into a series of quick swirls of limb and dress. Children picked up the mood and moved around to the music, jumping excitedly in little kangaroo hops or swinging each other around in monkey grips. Parents danced with children, women danced with women, couples swapped partners and reswapped. Those too old, too young or just too shy to join in stood around the hall watching. Most were tapping their feet in time to the music. The day which had started so tense had gladly dropped its cover.

Old man Parker was the first, and not the last, to fall victim to the slippery floor. His tumble into the sawdust was a noisy affair but cushioned by his natural padding. His wife put up a shriek of laughter, followed by the other women, until at last even the shopkeeper himself had to smile about it.

With all the energy and movement, the hall became very close. They tried to open the windows shutters but discovered they were nailed shut. The doors were opened and the dancers, flushed with the mood of the place, drifted out into the cool before the call of the music lured them back inside.

'The gentlemen may now remove their coats,' Tom Sayers called out.

'Thank goodness,' came a nearby female whisper. 'Have you seen the dandruff on their collars? Ugh!'

A few of the men chose to loosen their ties as well. The women swept up the damp strands of their hair and fanned at their faces with reddened hands. The bride had loosened her waistband and her high-heeled shoes were dangling in her hand. Her headpiece and veil were sitting crookedly and she was wearing the widest smile of anyone.

I could not see the Parker boy inside the hall, and then I realised I could not see any of the youths dancing. They were to be found behind the hall, sheltering behind a car and downing the contents of beer cans.

'It's all right.' I could see their alarm at my approach. 'It's all right. But it'll cost you a beer.' The can pulled out from underneath a rug was warm, but welcome. We cast our eyes everywhere, alert to the first sight of a stranger and ready to down cans quickly if it happened.

'Hey, listen,' one of the group hissed. Beer cans were held, frozen. 'It's the bloody Bridal Waltz.'

Startled, the Parker boy dropped his can and shot off back up to the hall. He skidded to a stop, bent down to check his fly was done up and then sped on. His mate carrying his bow tie and suit coat caught up with him just before he reached the hall, and the pair of them fussed around with the clothes for a moment before he was pushed inside.

By the time the rest of us sauntered in, the band was taking a break. The hall was alive with talk and milling bodies. Old man Parker stood by the door and grabbed my arm as I passed.

'I think I promised you a beer somewhere in all of this,' he said. 'But I suppose I'm a bit late,' he added, looking at the youths trying to look nonchalant and inconspicuous as they slid back into the hall. 'But I will tell you that I still owe you something.' He did not look at me as he spoke. 'I believe you've had a big part in all of this and ... er ... his mother and me, we're grateful.'

'Thank you.'

'Yeh.' He gave a relieved sigh. 'Well, I just thought I'd tell you. Are you going to join in the barn dance? My youngest girl, Amelia, she likes the old progressive barn dance ...'

Standing behind him was a spindly-limbed creature of no more than fourteen years. She had long, thin hair and a mouth you just knew would open to reveal buck-teeth and braces.

The soft, dark evening settled in and the band struck up the last bracket of songs as I danced into the night with my prize.

Now You See Him

In the field of human endeavour there was never a day more momentous than that when Nigs finished the tablecloths for Engels Café. If foul language and intensity of effort are the hallmarks of efficiency, the seven gingham squares should have been finished many weeks ago.

Nigs, equipped with a broken-down treadle machine, and hampered by a lack of tailoring skills, had to battle hard at the task. He swore at broken threads, he cursed at broken needles, he thumped that gallant old machine in desperation so many times that he was more often a mechanic than a seamstress. He had attempted hand-sewing the hems and finished with huge, ham-fisted and loopy stitching that you could have poked several fingers through. It takes only small things to push men into the depths of emotional instability. Those tablecloths were not large.

Dianne had taken the sad results of his labour gently aside and reworked them. She was becoming a frequent visitor to the café, and a familiar friend of Nigs.

By now, I assumed, they were lovers. I wondered if it was a politic acquaintance, but she seemed untroubled by the consequences. Lovers, while not blind to folly, see all things selectively.

For her efforts, and for my passing interest in the project, we were invited to a party unfurling the cloths. We winked to each other as Nigs flapped them around with a flourish.

'Tra-rah!' he sang in triumph, flagging down the last cloth like a magician in performance. 'Never before . . . and never again!'

We applauded loudly.

'Bravo,' said Dianne. 'A job well done.'

'Thank you, thank you, fans,' he replied, with the deepest of theatrical bows. When Nigs was this far into the suds he was far more entertaining; sobriety just doesn't suit some people.

'And for my next trick . . .' He reached for his bottle of beer and finished it with a hearty swig. Then he grabbed the empty glass in his hand, tightened his fist and shut his eyes in the exertion of crushing it like a can.

'No!' cried Dianne, alarmed at the risk.

Keeping his face screwed up with the effort, he opened the palm of his hand and then his eyes and allowed himself a long, sly smile. 'Nice to know you care,' he said.

I believe – but I can't be certain – that Dianne blushed.

'And now,' he continued, 'not only . . . but also.' He poised with an upraised finger pushed to his lips. 'Shut your eyes,' he told us. There was a scuffling noise, a heavy thud and then the order, 'Open your eyes now.'

A large, and unhemmed, cloth covered a tall upright object on the counter. 'Madam, if you please . . .' He escorted Dianne to its side with a polite bow and an airy wave.

'Only if you hold my glass,' she said.

'Honoured,' he said, taking it and drinking it.

'Speech! Speech!'

'Unaccustomed as I am . . .' she began.

'Don't believe it,' said Nigs in a hoarse stage whisper. 'Screws like a combine harvester.'

'. . . I am honoured to be asked,' said Dianne, darting her eyes toward Nigs, 'to perform this duty. Performance being something that others in this room may know little about . . .' She gave a wicked and self-satisfied grin. 'I undertake this task willingly,' she continued. 'And I, er . . .' Her words ran out. 'I need inspiration.'

'Have another drink.'

'Thank you.' She stared balefully at her empty glass. 'All I have to say is' – she gripped a corner of the cloth and whipped it aside – 'God bless her and all who sail in her. What the hell is it?'

She stood back, cocking her head one way and then the other. It was made of plaster and made passing references to sculpture . . . not all of them polite. It had ears, several of them, protruding from unlikely angles in unfamiliar places. If it was a face, then it was that of some unfortunate who had lost the fight with a runaway chain-saw.

'You mean you don't know who it is? You can't see?' Nigs sounded genuinely crushed.

'Not really. Not immediately,' said Dianne.

'Is it a bust?' I asked.

'Of someone famous?'

'A man?'

'Philistines.' Nigs had lost his good humour. He turned the statue slightly to afford us a better, but no clearer, view. He had trouble with its weight. 'There, can't you see now?'

Dianne pulled the air in through her teeth and looked at me uncertainly. I rubbed my nose and looked hard at the floor.

'All right, all right.' Nigs raised his hands in surrender. 'It's subjective, I grant you. Highly subjective. But it's Art . . . you must see that, surely.'

'Oh yes, Art.' I laughed with sudden relief.

'Art who?' Dianne asked.

Nigs turned ruddy high around the cheekbones, and I almost became uneasy in his huge presence. 'This is Art of the Proletariat,' he said. 'This is Socialist Art for the cultural enjoyment of the masses. I plan to establish a whole gallery of it.' He struck a pose between the coffee machine and his inaugural masterpiece. 'I have a dream,' he began. 'A dream of art of the people, by the people and for the people – removed from the capitalistic cloisters of galleries and placed among the people. Art shall be made available to the tired and the weary, the downtrodden masses, the huddled . . . how does the rest of it go?' He paused to remember and to wet his throat. 'And all of it overlooked by the man himself, Engels, the greatest modern philosopher.' He gave the statue an affectionate slap. It didn't budge.

'That's Engels?' Dianne did not bother to disguise her incredulity.

'A subjective interpretation, of course,' said Nigs. 'Of course.' She sounded unconvinced. 'Where did you find it?'

'Such things are not just found,' Nigs said haughtily. 'I commissioned it.'

'You paid money for it?'

'Banks don't take kindly to sea-shells any more,' I interjected.

'You shut up,' said Dianne. I returned my concentration to the floor boards.

'I commissioned it from a friend,' said Nigs. 'He's really committed...'

'And so he should be,' said Dianne. 'Or certified.'

'He's taken on interpretations of socialism in mixed medias. He really pushed back frontiers and he was just the man to capture the essence of socialist inspiration in the form of its greatest practitioner.'

I stared hard at the disembodied face. Inspiration leaves a hard and stormy mark on some people.

Dianne relaxed a little and surveyed the worked from all angles. 'I suppose it's too late to send it back,' she muttered, and gave it a long, last look. 'I still think it's ugly.'

'They said that of Henry Moore's work,' Nigs said.

'I think that's ugly too.'

When she strode into my office the next Tuesday morning, dragging the hapless Vivian behind her, Dianne was a study in determination. She flopped down into a chair, banging the desk with her fist.

'Good morning, Dianne.'

'Good morning? I'm furious. I'm livid. I want to see justice.'

'Something wrong in the paper?' I went to close the door.

'No, no. But they can't do this, damn it,' she exploded. Vivian climbed on to my chair and started worrying around with the telephone. 'This is corruption,' she said. 'The whole stinking mess of our society.'

I knew who she'd been talking to. 'What's the matter?'

She held her forehead, closed her eyes and took some slow, deep breaths. Vivian burrowed through the papers on my desk, crumpling them into a ball and pushing them by the fistful into his mouth.

First of all, I want to make it clear that I haven't got a personal set against Tilson. I'm not slinging mud, and I don't like telling tales. But this is corruption.'

'Right.'

'Last night,' she went on, 'last night I was driving back with Nigs along the Tingalla road – not too far out of town. It was about eleven-thirty, I suppose. Vivian was asleep in the back of the car and we were just talking quietly about this and that when we passed a car stopped by the side of the road. Not only was it stopped, it was in the ditch. We thought they might be in trouble, so we turned around and went back to see if they needed any help.'

'Right,' I said, gently prising Vivian's pudgy little fingers away from next week's race fields.

'So we went up to the car. Its engine was still running, the lights were on and the window was wound down. There was just one man sitting in it, slumped over the wheel. God! I thought he was dead. We got a torch and when we shone it inside the car – do you know who it war? Old man Tilson! I nearly died! I thought he must have had a heart attack or something.'

'I saw him in the street this morning. He looked alive to me.'

'I'm not surprised,' she continued. 'That man has nine lives. Vivian – stop chewing that newspaper. Anyway, we were worried. I mean, I was genuinely worried for a fellow human being regardless of who it was. We shook him, we took his pulse, we slapped his face. He was alive but we couldn't bring him around. And stink! His breath was like an east wind through a brewery. I tell you, he was so drunk he was catatonic.'

'How could you tell the difference?'

She stopped a moment, and actually relaxed into a slight smile. Vivian decided to join in the fun and started pulling the loose keys off my typewriter.

'So we were standing there wondering what the hell to do. I mean – do we leave him in his car? He'd probably still be drunk when he woke up and started driving again. Do we pull him out of the car and take him home? Do we call an ambulance, or what? So we're standing there a while talking this over, and, far off, we see a pair of headlights coming this way. Another car's coming and we think "Good, they can help us load him into our car and take him home." He's no light-weight and the pair of us would have had a battle just to lift him by ourselves – even Nigs.

'Well, as this car gets closer we see that it is, in face, a police car, and when it stopped who should get out but, oh, I've forgotten his name... The sergeant...'

'Lawson?'

'Yes. Big bloke. Moustache. Well, he flashes a torch in our faces and asks what we're doing there. It was like the Spanish

Inquisition, I tell you. The third degree,' she said. 'He must have thought we were up to no good, I don't know. And we just tell him that we stopped to offer help. It was the decent thing to do, you see.'

'Yes.'

'So he strides past us and looks around the car, checking for damage, or anything missing I suspect. We tell him that the driver is old man Tilson and he's three sheets to the wind and shouldn't be driving. He flashes the torch inside the car very quickly and continues walking around the outside, checking to see if all the wheels are there and what have you. So we ask him, "What are you going to do with him?" – Tilson, I mean. "Are you going to call an ambulance, or what?" And he turns to us and says, "Why? There's no one in that car." I told him of course there was, it was old man Tilson. I could see him there in front of my very eyes, slumped over the wheel like a sack of flour. But that cop just saying there was no one in the car. I tell you, I was starting to lose my temper at this stage. So I asked him about the engine and the lights being on and he suddenly swings his torch into my face and says, "I don't know what you mean. The lights are off and the engine's off too." And I tell him, of course they're off because we'd turned them off. And then he asks us if we've touched the car and of course we say we had. And then' – she leaned forward – 'then he tells us that the car is not only driverless but legally abandoned. Not only that, but he tells us that we've committed an offence by interfering with an abandoned car – just by turning off the engine and the lights!'

'Hell.'

'Yes, I know. And that's when I really blew my top. I tell you. Nigs did too. And that's another thing... he asked the pair of us what we were doing out together at that time of night. It was like the Thought Police out of *Nineteen Eighty-four*. Big Brother is watching you, and all that. The cheek of the man! And then he went to take our names and addresses and asked if we both lived at the same place. I'm afraid I went completely off the deep end. The bastard was so taken aback that he put away his notebook and said he's just report it as an abandoned vehicle.'

'He said that, did he?'

'Yes,' she said, her voice assuming a high, thin, sarcastic

pitch. 'He said he would just report it as an abandoned vehicle and that he'd very kindly overlook us tampering with it. Out of the goodness of his heart! Such a kind man is Sergeant Lawson. And then he tells us to clear off. Just like that. Rude? I've never met a ruder man. And all last night I was stewing over it. I hardly slept at all. And I thought I'd report him to the police officials – but that wouldn't do much good, Nigs said. He reckons they're all just as corrupt. So I thought you could do something about it. You could expose this bastard and this corruption for the evil that it really is.'

She was panting from the exertion. Even Vivian was silent and watched her closely.

'But I suppose your paper wouldn't print something as controversial as that, would it?' she said.

I sat on the edge of the desk. 'I'm willing to give it a go,' I said. 'I'm not going to ramble on about editorial control, but you should understand that there's a lot of hurdles to clear.'

She nodded. 'I'll stand by my claims. Nigs will too. We'll sign a statutory declaration about it if we must.'

'A stat. dec. has to be signed by the local Justice of the Peace,' I said.

'Well, fine. Who's that?'

'Tilson.'

'Oh,' she said, sitting quietly back in her chair. She took some time to recover. 'Well, I came here just to tell you what happened. It's riled me so much.'

'I understand. Give me some time to sniff around. I have to verify the fact officially from the police, because your claim brings the whole thing up as a police matter of some seriousness. It's nothing personal against you, but I've got to check these details because this is the law we're dealing with.' I searched her face for a reaction.

'Tilson probably won't remember a thing about it. It's probably commonplace for him,' she said.

'Right, now you're starting to understand the problems,' I said. 'And I'm going to have to check it with the police. Sergeant Lawson told you he would report it as an abandoned car?'

'Yes.'

'Right. Then that's what I'm after. I'll give you a call if I get anywhere with it.'

'Thank you,' she said. 'And thank you for listening. Vivian, Vivian, get out of that rubbish bin.'

'Adventurous little tyke, isn't he.' I chose my words carefully.

'Yes. It's all an important part of his learning experience,' she said.

'Glad to help. If you're not careful, he might turn into a reporter and then your troubles will really start.'

I spent some time retrieving the scattered pages of the sports story I had been typing. Some damp, crumpled balls turned out to be important results sheets. After reassembling the loose letters back on the typewriter keyboard I found the K and the V missing for all time.

'Good morning, John, How are you coping?'

Constable Orchard looked up from his desk as I entered. Way out here, where folk were peaceful souls, the force of the law operated from one small room, one wooden desk and a filing system cardboard boxes stuffed to overflowing.

'How am I? Fair to muddling I guess,' he said.

'This place isn't sending you around the twist, is it?'

'No, no,' he said. 'It's just that the mirror answered back this morning.'

Sergeant Lawson strolled in and welcomed me in his traditional manner – 'No rapes, no murders and the end of the world has been postponed until next week's races. How can I help you?'

'I'm looking for an abandoned car.'

'You and whose auntie... we get stacks of abandoned cars out here.'

'Just wondering if you have a report of one out on the Tingalla road, about eleven-thirty last night.'

'Can't think of one.' His face was impassive.

'I believe it may have been reported.'

'Can't remember seeing one. Can you, John?'

Constable Orchard shook his head and left the room. Well trained, that one.

'Can you check for me?' I asked.

He looked at me a moment and said, 'Sure.' He scoured the incident book, laying it flat on the desk for me to see. 'No, nothing here.'

'Perhaps it's in the MOs.'

'Doubt it. Not the sort of thing you file there. But I'll have a look for you.' He leafed through the sheets. 'Did you get that theft of a letterbox outside young Michaelson's place?'

I nodded.

'No, nothing here about an abandoned car,' he said. 'Where did you say it was?'

'On the Tingalla road.'

'Do you know exactly whereabouts? It could have been outside our police district.'

'I don't think so,' I said. 'Close to town was the report I got.'

'Whereabouts did you hear this from?' he asked.

'Oh, just around,' I said airily.

'Around,' he echoed softly, turning to look out of the window. 'Well, perhaps they'd like to come into the police station and tell us. If it's a police matter then we'll deal with it fully. We get a lot of people tampering with abandoned cars, fiddling with them, leaving fingerprints.' He paused, and added, looking directly at me, 'They're usually blow-ins, not locals, people from Melbourne. Would you know anything more about this alleged abandoned car, then?'

'Probably about as much as you do,' I said.

'But I know nothing about it.'

'There you go, then.'

'There you go.'

Lot 57

The cool morning had swelled out into a good-natured afternoon. A benign sun overlooked the land, amazing the earth out of its winter huddle.

At the wheel of his ute – which was still defying fate and the law – Nigs was relatively at peace and was not struggling too hard with the Human Condition. The flat, straight road out to the Michaelson place threw up no driving challenges and Nigs, unable to endure long, silent spaces, was talking.

'That housemate of yours didn't sound very committed to me,' he said. 'What did you say his name was?'

'Tam.'

'But then, he is an artist,' Nigs continued, showing his misplaced reverence for that fickle breed. 'So I reckon he must be with us. Don't you think?'

'You can never be sure about anything, Nigs.'

'And he didn't seem very committed to the Party,' he mused.

I said nothing but considered how committed anyone could be the morning after an evening such as Tam's. Any parties on his mind were most assuredly unpolitic.

There was a dark hint of suspicion to Nig's disturbingly high voice. 'You don't think he's a reactionary, do you?'

'I don't think so.'

'Oh Christ – he's not a Maoist, is he?' Nigs sounded genuinely alarmed.

'I doubt that,' I said. 'Politically uncommitted, I suppose.'

'You mean a swinging voter?' Nigs brightened. 'If we could get him along to a few meetings, we might just hook him. We might pin him down.'

'Oh, I wouldn't do that,' I said, and then – for no good

reason – added, 'He's an epileptic. Can't take too much excitement,' and gave a knowing look.

'Oh, so he's disabled. Or is that disadvantaged? I forget which term you're supposed to use,' said Nigs. 'In any case, I understand,' he concluded, as if Tam's fictional affliction should absolve him from all responsibilities of democracy.

It didn't take many silent minutes before he was at it again. 'I reckon old man Tilson is only waking up now to the fight he has on his hands. I bet he's realising that it's not all plain sailing.' And he smiled to himself. 'She's a game one, isn't she?' He did not wait for my reaction. 'And intelligent too. I bet he didn't realise what hit him. She's certainly got balls – in a non-sexist sort of way, of course. Don't you think?'

I fudged an answer. My position was a most uncomfortable one, for I was now to be held in suspicion by both sides and bound to be accused by either of favouritism or bias. It was difficult, like straddling a fence and only then discovering it to be electrified – at peril but afraid to move one way or another. Coward that I was, I recalled one of Pat's prized explanations. 'If one side hates my guts and the other thinks I'm a contemptible worm, then I must be doing something right.'

Nigs sniffed. 'Strange, that's the way I've always approached campaigning.' And he gave me one of his big, idiotic grins that pulled the mass of his beard up to his ears.

Cars were clustered as flies to the carrion as we pulled up outside the Michaelson's place. A keen and caustic eye would have lighted upon the scavengers searching through the auction lots. A bitter mouth would have murmured 'vultures'. But things were far too practical for regret.

The Michaelson's place had, for decades, faded from profitability. Even after the seemingly senseless equations of depreciation, subsidy and fixed assets, things were no better. The many sons of the family had the intelligence to scatter further than the reaches of family influence. One or two had even shifted into the city suburbs. They were crows of another kind – waiting for the final carve-up they considered their birthright.

The old man's harvest was an exceedingly bitter one. He struggled, but there was no denying that his arthritis coupled with the injuries, seen and unseen, he had scored up in the

Owen Stanley Ranges were choking the whole enterprise into a protracted death.

At least, they said, he came to farming late. There was no grand tradition on the land for this family – only a soldier settler who carved out a rough living from the dry and heartless land he had earned in defending it in 1942. The land was better sold, they said. They would retire, man and wife, into a flat in the town – but not without shedding the fittings of their lives. There were belongings loved and long-possessed, sometimes long-forgotten in their familiarity, and now on public offer.

There was a cruel detachment to the catalogue that listed the detritus of their marriage, their breeding and their farm. 'Radiator, one bar not working,' – you could almost hear their annoyance unleased upon the faulty electricals. 'Six crystal goblets' – a wedding present perhaps left treasured and untouched save for christenings and funerals. Rabbit traps, baby baths, five pounds of assorted nails, binding twine. There were boxes smelling of mothballs and faded bags of lavender, smelling of must or rust or just plain age. There was no denying the sadness of it, nor scorning the opportunity.

Ranged along the drive were items of farm machinery of ancient vintage and doubtful efficiency – but doubtless of enduring interest for men whose minds appreciated such things. These lots must have been collected over the years, perhaps from other auctions, with all good intentions of restoration when time allowed. And from here they would probably be sold and shifted to other sheds of the district. Here they would remain, untouched, to gather another layer of dust and chaff glued together into an oily grime. These men were not by nature optimists, but this was their folly and it was indigenous to farming regions. It was folly made acceptable by its frequency.

The women pursued their own passions with no less dedication. They desired, but never bidded, not with their own hands. They used a very refined form of telepathy, a persuasion that was heeded by their spouses who then activated the bidding. The links came alive as each item was held aloft by the auctioneer, and grew most frenzied, by proxy, when fine china was proffered. Anything bearing a floral pattern unleashed a tide of hurried bids by the husbands, elbowed by the wives keen to shoulder away competitors.

The instinct to hoard was something sprung out of hardship,

an experience not unknown to these farming families. Playing hard upon these sentiments, the auctioneer sprinkled his patter with comment. 'Lot 28,' he intoned in a monotone of unbroken soliloquy. 'Lot 28 and what we have here is a dozen redgum fenceposts, finished and rotproofed these are. Good solid redgum which will not rot even when you do. Always handy to have some of these around the place for replacement or for new fencing around Mum's garden to keep the stock away from her cabbages or what have you. Always useful, redgum posts, and so now I'll take offers and open the bidding . . .' It was a fast-flung and rapid commentary on the needs of life – even if those needs were not, at first, obvious.

'. . . and seven yards of chicken wire with no rust and no breaks. As good as the day it was made, this chicken wire. Seven yards on offer here and useful for fencing, or for planting trellises or just for wrapping up and stacking in a corner until you need it . . .' The spell was seamless and fluid, and devilishly inviting.

'. . . carpet underfelt, that's what we've got here, underfelt for a carpet, and there's a lot of it too. How much have we got here? Enough for three rooms at least, I'd say. Three big rooms too. It's no use laying new carpet if you just stick the tired old underfelt back – no use at all. This way you can do a proper job cheaply – very cheaply. Always useful for other things too, underfelt. Good for lining plant beds, dog kennels, babies' bottoms – you name it . . .'

For one impractical moment I considered the possibility. I didn't even own a dog. The lot drew slow and reluctant bidding, however. The inspiration of the auctioneer had fallen on hard ground and stony resolve – a reception he took with good grace, throwing in a small rug and knocking the offering down for a low price. 'A bargain price, ladies and gentlemen, a real bargain.'

Even as he spoke he pulled the next lot on to his bench. He seemingly functioned without pause and did not need to draw breath. 'And don't forget there's cups of tea so nicely prepared by the ladies of the hospital auxiliary in the porch. Very good value afternoon tea they are serving. Now, what have we here? An assortment of drill bits . . .'

And so it continued. He was a fuse slow-burning and steady, unflappable in the rush of bids and accustomed to the manner of parts where money was earned seasonally and spent with reluctance.

Looming large over the afternoon teas, Mrs Tilson dealt out cups with the manner of a veteran. Her muscular arms were designed for lifting heavy teapots, her fingernails clipped blunt and kept clinically clean, her hands softened by endless plunging into washing-up water. She must have been a Girl Guide before she joined the auxiliary, and the Red Cross and the other worthy causes to which her aid was directed. She was as adept a caterer as she was a shrewd judge of the politics of these groups. And she had a habit of bossiness. As a result she fairly ruled the town. And this was to be expected, as the wife of old man Tilson and matriarch of that distinguished family.

She was such an old hand at this that none of her assistants dared vary from her instructions. None of the customers risked dissension, either. When she barked 'Have some milk', it was less of an invitation than a command. She possessed a voice of stentorian tones, and when she cast out an order, it was delivered with the impact of half a bullock slapped down hard on a slab.

Before her, the tea-cups were lined in military precision and filled to a universal level.

'Do you have any coffee?' asked Nigs.

'No,' she intoned, stonily.

'Well then, I won't have anything,' he said, and wandered back to the bidding.

She regarded his departure with distrust. 'I don't know what people like that are doing here,' she thought to herself in a voice loud enough to carry.

'He's after an urn for his restaurant,' I said, exchanging some coins for a cup of tea. I suppose I hoped that the explanation would prove his honest intent. 'There's one coming up for sale later this afternoon.'

'Is that so?' Mrs Tilson was interested. She looked at Nigs with barbs. 'We need a new urn for the auxiliary. The heating element has almost packed up on our old one.' She handed me a teaspoon. 'And the hospital auxiliary is such a deserving cause – don't you think? Sugar? Milk?'

I tried to warn him after that, but Nigs seemed unconvinced by Mrs Tilson's worthiness.

'She's still a fat old cow,' he muttered. 'And a capitalist.'

'Come on, Nigs. It's only an urn.'

'It's not just an urn. This is a struggle of the classes against those acquisitive fat cats.'

I moved away from him slightly, and looked around me. Mrs Tilson had abandoned the afternoon tea stand and was locked in discussion with her husband. I saw them turn to watch Nigs and I had a good idea what they were plotting. I moved further away. They gave a look that should have set off warning sirens in any right-thinking mind. Nigs determinedly avoided their gaze.

I watched old man Tilson shift through the crowd, speaking to the occasional town worthy. He had his head bowed and his back turned. From a distance he caught the eye of the auctioneer's sidekick and motioned him outside. Nigs chose not to see these machinations.

It was nothing more prepossessing than an urn, a faithful worker wrought in metal that wasn't polished, and plastic that was worn. When it was lifted aloft as Lot 57 it commanded attention as if it were fashioned in gold from the hands of Cellini. For all the interest it commanded, this setting could just as well have been a plush London saleroom as the wide verandah of the Michaelson place.

Nigs did not appear to notice the ring of open space that had cleared about him. I stood at the back of the crowd, repelled and yet drawn by the fearsome inevitability of it all.

The auctioneer opened the bidding with his eyes cemented firmly on the heavens. 'Ten dollars, I want ten dollars – yes, I have ten dollars, I want twenty. Do I have twenty?' Nigs's head inclined a little and he caught the eye of the auctioneer.

'I am looking for thirty, do we have thirty? I need a bid of thirty dollars.' His eyes scanned the crowd and lighted upon a bid, I could not see from whom. He cried out jubilantly, 'Thirty, over here we have thirty. And now I have a bid for forty, forty dollars.'

'Fifty,' yelled Nigs.

'Fifty,' cried the auctioneer, springing back like a taut sapling.

'Fifty-five,' came a call from Forbes.

'Fifty-six,' called Nigs.

'Sixty,' yelled old man Parker.

'Sixty-two.' Nigs edged up the bids, only now he looked as if he was suffering.

'Sixty-five.' It was the voice of old man Tilson, unrelenting and unrepentant. It was, after all, his home town advantage.

'Do we have seventy?' The auctioneer could not believe his good fortune.

The urn was becoming something more than just a domestic appliance – something far more profound. It had come to represent civic pride, and its ownership would be a symbol of dominance in the town. Nigs had never been made very welcome as a newcomer, and now, by assaulting the sanctity of the Nooweep Hospital auxiliary, he was putting himself beyond the pale. He was just too pig-headed, too stubborn and too intent on assaulting the ruling classes to stop. He bid again.

'Yes, I have seventy,' said the auctioneer. Nigs looked pleased with himself.

'Eighty,' came the call.

'Eighty-one,' yelled back Nigs.

'Eighty-two.'

'Eighty-three.' The contesting bids were flying in from all directions.

'Eighty-four.'

'Eighty-five.'

The auctioneer rested his hands for a moment. 'Gentlemen, I know how to count. Let's be serious about these bids and not get too petty.' He straightened up, took a short pause and recommenced. 'I have eighty-five in that corner,' and he pointed to Nigs.

'One hundred.' The voice of Dr Forbes was edged with finality. All noise, all movement froze for a moment, and even the auctioneer was stilled in surprise. He retrieved his voice. 'I have one hundred dollars – one hundred – is there any advance on one hundred dollars?'

The line of Nigs's massive jaw was shifting slowly backwards and forwards. His face looked white and pulled tight in anger, his lips were moving softly beneath the great russet brush of his beard.

'One hundred I have. One hundred.' The auctioneer sensed his indecision – and his bloody-mindedness. 'I have one hundred once...' He lowered his hand. 'Twice...' His hand hovered for the faintest of regrets. Then he slapped the bench top. 'Sold.'

Nig turned around and stalked through the parting crowd.

He walked off with a stiff back and rigid limbs. I found him at the back of the hayshed kicking at a clump of sedge grass. It loosed its hold of the earth and sailed far through the air.

'Aren't they just the mightiest of mobs?' he muttered low and dangerously and turned his fury on to another clump of sedge. 'Mobs? Mobsters, more likely. Muggers. Capitalist muggers.' He kicked so hard that the second clump also lost its grip and flew away in a scatter of soil. 'Pigs, pigs, pigs.'

'It's hardly a major defeat,' I suggested. 'It's only a tea-urn. Not a trophy.' I didn't believe my own words.

'Bloody pigs.'

'You're being a very sore loser.'

'And they're being... being... just bastards. The lot of them.'

'Calm down.'

'Be buggered.'

'You're being childish. You saw the warnings. You ignored them. You lost. You had your chance.'

'Chance? You mean fat chance.' He thrust his hands deeply into his pockets and angrily jangled his keys and loose change. 'They were only out to get me.'

'You gave them cause.'

'I needed an urn for the restaurant.'

'So did the hospital.'

'But the hospital's big enough. The restaurant hasn't got the sort of friends that the hospital has.'

'Certainly not after today it hasn't. You've done your project a lot of harm today.'

'I couldn't give a stuff.'

'You don't mean that. You shouldn't have upset them, you know. They run the town.'

'And you're their bloody little lap-dog.' He was looming over me with threat tightening at his shoulders and forearms. I did not look higher than his chest, fearing eye contact would unleash an angry swipe. I could hear a hiss in his voice. 'You little traitor. You bloody mangy little turncoat.' I started to back away.

'Good news, good news,' Mrs Tilson called as she waddled up to me. She cast Nigs a short, sharp glance and pushed closer to me – not a breath's distance from my face. 'Dr Forbes bought the urn. Did you see? And he has donated it to the hospital auxiliary.' It was sheer, unabashed gall. Nigs turned and began to walk away. 'Out of the blue he bid for it, and asked me if the hospital could do with it.' She was evidently enjoying herself. 'So of course, I said we'd be delighted with the gift. The hospital auxiliary is such a deserving cause, don't you think?'

I saw Nigs driving out on to the road with a maddened roar. I would have to get a lift back into town.

The Voice of the Turtle

Sounds of voices merged with the blast of music issuing out of my house. All the lights were on and there was a confusion of cars blocking my driveway. Shapes of bodies weaved past the windows. I counted three and wondered if I really wanted to attend an impromptu party tonight. After a day of telephone and typewriters I had been looking forward to an evening of television for company and monosyllabic grunts for conversation.

In the living-room Tam, Nigs and Pat were shifting around carrying beer bottles. The television was on, the record-player was on and the radio was on. The terrified budgie flapped wildly in its upended cage. Tam was trying to balance a glass on his forehead wavered, and jumped back as it fell and rolled across the carpet. Nigs was sitting at my typewriter, stabbing at the keys like a chicken pecking for grain. With his other hand he reached for the ashtray, missed and stubbed out his cigarette on the table. He didn't notice. 'Your turn,' he said, jumping up and launching himself in a flying leap on to the couch.

Pat took the seat at the typewriter and stared a while at the paper, blinking a lot. Then he launched into a flurry of fingers, flourishing at the end of a line. Then it was Tam's turn.

'Thassnot fair,' Tam said. ''Snot,' he continued, sticking his finger up his nose for explanation and wiping it elaborately along the table. 'You guys get the easy lines. I'm the muggins who has to find the rhymes. Turtle, look at that. Turtle, who wrote that? How the hell can I finish that couplet? What rhymes with turtle for Chrissakes?'

'Aurtle, burtle, curtle, durtle, eurtle...' Nigs muttered, as he idly peeled the label from his beer bottle. 'Furtle, that sounds as if it could be a word. Furtle . . .'

'Ah yes, we had one of those in the back yard,' said Pat. 'But the wheels fell off.'

'Would you like a twist of lemon in your furtle?' giggled Nigs. 'How many capitalist pigs does it take to change a furtle?'

'How many?'

'None, my good man. I'll pay you to do it for me.'

'The dictionary doesn't list any furtle,' said Pat. 'No . . . no furtles. But there's a furuncular going cheap.'

'Furunculars don't go "cheep",' said Nigs.

'They are those little cable cars going up the sides of mountains,' said Tam. 'Furuncular railways.'

'You mean funucular,' said Nigs.

'And funuculoo to you, too,' said Tam.

'You're both wrong. It's funicular,' said Pat.

'Funiculee, funicular, funiculee, funicular-ha-ha-ha-ha . . .' Tam was trying to yodel.

'Kirtle rhymes with turtle,' said Pat. 'It was something they used in the Middle Ages, I think.'

'You mean before penicillin?'

'You mean before unmarried mothers?'

'Who needs abortion when you've got a kirtle?' said Nigs, giggling with a noise like a blocked s-bend.

'And you wouldn't need abortion if it wasn't for that other nasty habit,' said Pat in mock-seriousness.

'You mean sniffing bicycle seats,' gasped Tam, clutching at his heart. 'Oh no. I never knew. Is it too late?'

'Hey, listen, listen.' Pat was leafing through the dictionary. ' "Xyloidine – chemical explosive formed through the treatment of vegetable fibre with nitric acid." I knew a drink like that once.'

'Bugger all that. Read us out the dirty bits,' Tam said. 'Words like bum and breast. Let's relive our childhood.'

'Come off it,' said Nigs. 'You were never a child. You were just something the surgeons put together with all the offcuts.'

'And you were obviously a homesick abortion,' said Tam. 'What went wrong? Couldn't they find a loophole in your birth certificate?'

They all thought it very funny and exploded into laughter. Tam rolled on to his back and spun around, kicking his legs like a dying blowfly. The whoops of their laughter were punctuated by occasional draughts from their bottles. Nigs inhaled some of the liquid and spat it out in a fit of coughing. The white foam clung to his beard and dribbled down his shirt front. They all chortled like schoolboys.

'Ah, this is the life. Wouldn't be dead for quids,' Pat said.

'Are good little socialists allowed to be decadent?' Tam asked.

'Good living is not the birthright of the ruling classes. The proletariat are just as entitled to good things. The Leninist ideology states that . . .'

'Put a sock in it, Nigs,' said Pat. 'How's this bloody poem of ours coming along? Are we going to knock the boots off Dante or just dip a toe into the *Inferno*?'

'Abandon hope all ye who enter here,' Tam intoned. 'I knew a girl like that once. We used to call her Billingsgate Market because she always smelled of . . .'

'So what about this bloody poem then?' asked Nigs. 'Are we almost ready to launch it on Grub Street? Who'll handle the sale of the film rights?'

'You've seen the movie, you've read the book, you've heard the soundtrack, you're wearing the T-shirt, now taste the cocktail.' Tam's arms were waving about. 'Next thing they'll be making it in pill form.' The budgie huddled further back into its cage. 'Deathless prose.' His voice has dropped to a hushed reverence. 'Deathless prose I hold here in my hands, dear friends. A masterpiece of form and imagery.' He stared at the piece of paper, swaying on his feet. 'Pity someone can't spell.'

He cleared his throat, pushed a discarded bottle top into his mouth and, with perfectly-rounded vowels, began to read in Queen's English:

> *'There was swishing in the haystacks,*
> *And in the light of morn*
> *Came the sound of threshing bodies*
> *Writhing in the corn.*
> *And the bringing in of sheaves . . .'*

'. . . And the donning of the sheaths,' interrupted Nigs.

'Gentlemen, this is poetry. Doggerel night is next Friday,' said Tam. 'May I continue?'

'Please.'

'... And the bringing in of sheaves,
And the sowing of wild oats,
And the twitting of the birds,
And the squealing of riled stoats.
All swelled over the earth like the voice of the turtle...'

He dropped the sheet to the floor. 'And there's that bloody turtle again,' he said. 'That last line doesn't even scan properly.'

'Myrtle. Myrtle, that rhymes with turtle,' Nigs offered. 'And kirtle. And furtle.'

Tam snapped his fingers and returned to the typewriter, plunging into it like a crazed wordsmith.

'... voice of the turtle. Dimly heard through tangled wood and matted myrtle.'

'But did Myrtle matter in that great Dawn of Life?' Pat smiled at his own word-play.

'Her mother must have thought so. She became somebody's wife,' said Nigs.

'Her father thought of little else, facing Daddy's old shotgun...'

'... staring ahead with resentful discretion...'

'... and dying all the while to run.'

'And so the moral of this tale, dear friends. If moralise one may...'

'... is to plough the field, not spill the seed whene'er you're making hay.'

The applause lasted a long time.

'What shall we call it?' Nigs asked over the din.

'I rather fancy "Pastorale",' Tam said.

'Very swanky,' said Nigs.

'Give or take a consonant,' Pat said.

They gagged and snorted on their bottles. Nigs kicked the budgie's cage. Pat danced a quick fandango around the rug, tripping over the coffee-table and sending the fruit-bowl flying.

'Allez oop, allez oop.' Tam picked up a couple of oranges and tried to juggle them. He fumbled and dropped one, ducking moments before another sailed over his head and splattered against the wall. The spray of pulp stuck to the paint, the juice dribbled down. A banana went airborne in retaliation. It hit the window and bounced off under the couch. From behind the heater Pat launched a light artillery attack and Waltham Cross grapes flew across the room.

'I bet Oscar Wilde never had as much fun as this,' said Nigs, ducking and twisting to avoid the barrage.

'He was always mixing his genders,' Tam added.

'Mixing them with pleasure,' said Pat. 'Truce, truce, I've run out of grapes. Come back, D. H. Lawrence. All is forgiven. Most, anyway.'

'Who wants another beer?' asked Nigs.

'Ooh, yes please,' Tam lisped, and lifted a lock of hair. 'Just a dab behind the ear please, sweetie.'

Nigs took a drink. He minced up to Tam with an exaggerated walk. Tam took delight in copying him. The pair of them burst into laughter at the sight of each other. Nigs wound his arm around Tam's shoulders and nuzzled into his neck. Tam only stopped laughing when he felt the trickle of warm bear run out of his ear and down his neck.

'Unsanitary moron,' he yelled, shaking his head like a wet spaniel. 'Don't you know Louis Pasteur died for the likes of you.'

'Was someone offering another beer?' asked Pat.

'If three men drank fifty bottles of beer – how many bottles would they remember drinking by the morning?' Nigs pondered.

'Was someone offering another beer?' Pat repeated.

'Voulez-vous un autre bottle de piss, m'sieur?' asked Nigs with a deep and elaborate bow.

'But of cour-r-r-se,' said Tam with a gutteral drag that sounded like a Gallic pissoir suffering a serious malfunction.

'If three men drank five bottles of brandy in an hour, would they... no, that's not right.' Nigs tried again. 'If three men...'

'... in a boat,' added Tam.

'In a boat?'

'Howsabout another beer?' said Pat.

'If three men in a boat drank...'

'If three drunks...'

'If three drunk boats... drunk... boats...'

'I need another beer,' yelled Pat. 'More beer! More beer!'

'It'll kill you,' said Tam, wagging a finger in his face. 'If I should die' – he turned on his heels and waltzed across the room – 'If I should die, think only this of me...'

'Codpiece.'

'If I should die 'twill be for lack of beer,' said Pat.

'If I should die, send God the invoice,' said Nigs.

'If I should die, please God, make it before her boyfriend finds out,' said Tam.

'I think I'd like to end up in intensive care with an intravenous at one end linked up to a bedpan and another out the other end linked to a bottle of single malt,' said Pat.

'You'd better specify which end's which,' said Tam.

'Besides, they'd have to put you into hospital,' said Nigs.

'For him it would have to be quarantine,' said Tam. 'Oh God. I feel sick.'

'Sick sick?' asked Nigs, suddenly very concerned.

'Just a bit wobbly.'

'For Chrissakes sit down then,' said Nigs, now looking wild-eyed. 'Lie down on the floor. Isn't that what you're supposed to do? Shall I phone for Dr Forbes?'

'What the . . . ?'

'Should I darken the room? Should I put a stick in your mouth?'

'He's not a bloody dog,' said Pat.

'Ssh . . .' said Nigs. 'He's having . . .'

'. . . His periods, don't tell me,' laughed Pat.

'What am I having?' said Tam.

'You know. One of your . . . fits, sort of,' Nigs said.

'What are you talking about?' said Tam.

'It's nothing to be ashamed of, you know.'

'What?'

'Epilepsy. Nothing wrong with it at all. Some of the best people have it. Caesar had it.'

'Epilepsy?'

'Yes. And VD too, I think.'

'VD?' Tam was shaking his head trying to comprehend. 'What makes you think I've got . . . ?'

I tiptoed as quietly as I could down the hall into my room and climbed into bed fully clothed. The prayer that I whispered had to do with the strength of the local bottled beer and its effect on the human memory the morning after.

Lost Sheep

Sheets of rain passed before the car's headlights, snuffing out the beams before they hit the road. The fat drops of water seemed to hang in lines. The spastic slap of the windscreen wipers raised a desperate sound against the battering of the water against the car. The windscreen was awash between each stroke and I drove slowly and fearfully.

Darkness had settled widely over the flat land, punctuated only rarely by the faint light from an isolated house. My own home seemed a world away, and there was a longing in me just to give up and go back there.

Easing off around a corner, I realised I had been driving for more than an hour, too intent on the dangers ahead to notice I had been grinding my teeth all the while. And as I slackened my grip on the steering wheel the muscles palsied after clutching white-knuckled for so long.

I was tired, cold and numbed into stupor.

Already the low-lying sections of the road were guttered with rivulets. The sandy sides were subsiding into the muddy swill of stormwater. At Gordon's Ford I lifted my foot and rolled the car slowly to the edge of the water washing over the road. It was perhaps a foot deep. It was not a danger itself for it still appeared to be moving sluggishly and would not wash the car off the road. But the road itself may already have started to sink in places, leaving a deep and unseen pothole. Stuck there with drowned electricals, the car would be a ripe victim for the rising waters, and I would have to abandon it.

I had told old man Gordon I'd call in that night, when he'd finished milking and would have time to talk. On the telephone he sounded reluctant and surly, like some swelling of mistrust was catching in his throat and stifling his words. He had farmed this country for all of his sixty-eight years, and from that heritage had acquired the taciturn manner of these parts. He would not tolerate fools, and I could only guess at his scorn if I failed to show up and offered an excuse of bad weather.

But my heart had left me. There was none of his spirit in me at any time and certainly far less now. I wanted out. I spun the wheel and shoved the car into reverse.

There was an odd feeling of weightlessness followed by a frightening lack of motion as I pushed the gears back and tried to swing the car forwards. A whine from the back wheels sent a shudder through the chassis, but the car still sat crippled.

The prayer I uttered was not silent as I realised I was now bogged beside a rising ford. With swelling panic I bashed into reverse and swung quickly into first gear, trying to cheat physics and free myself. Then I spun the wheel and repeated the action, hoping that bravado and sheer bloody-mindedness would cheat me clear. The car sent up another wail of protest.

Opening the door, I put one foot to the ground and accelerated hard with the other, trying to push and wriggle the car free. I heaved and strained but it was lodged fast, and within seconds I was soaked through. I hunted for makeshift wheel-jams, cursing myself for emptying the load of split logs I had collected for the fire last weekend. A canvas bag, a wallet, last week's paper – at least I had something to read. Remembering an old ploy, I went around the wheels levering off the trims. I piled two behind each rear tyre. Climbing back in the car I tried to reverse on to them for traction. The force of the spin sent them skidding into the darkness.

I howled at the wind that now set a chill through the dampness in me. Looking around, I saw no light but noticed instead a slight lift in the level of the water now washing stronger over the ford. I would have to leave the car there.

Locking it, I wondered what thieves would be about on a night like this, and set off back down the road. Without light it was difficult to judge the direction of the road, and I edged gingerly ahead fearing that the next step would lead me off the edge into a swollen roadside ditch. It was like being drunk without half the pleasure. Looking back after the first mile, I realised I had left the headlights on, and for an impractical moment almost considered going back to save the battery from draining power.

It must have been another two miles before I spotted a farmhouse sending a feeble light out into the dark. I walked quicker towards it, and by the time I reached the sweep of the gravel drive, I was running. I did not stop running until I reached the door and battered at it.

The light suffused in the frosted glass panel broke out as the door opened. I smelled wood-smoke and the lingering scent of an evening meal. A flat-faced woman with huge hips stood wedged in the light. I could not see much else.

She slammed the door shut. I could have wept, had I not been so furious. I pounded the door for a long time before it was opened again, this time by an old man casting a thin shadow.

'Could you help me, please? My car's bogged by Gordon's Ford and the water's rising.'

He seemed to stop and think a moment before stepping aside to show me into the house. 'I'll get my coat,' he said, and shuffled away.

I stepped inside, dripping over the scuffed linoleum. It was a kitchen full of clutter. The heavy black stove stood out as the only surface not littered with papers, clothes and household oddments. It was living-room, dining-room and kitchen all in one warm, close space. The long dining-table was covered with a stained cloth over which was spread last week's paper.

Two dogs lay around, lulled by the soporific warmth into ignoring a stranger. The old woman sat on a low chair, also ignoring me. She did not look up but sat darning the elbow of a jumper in large, clumsy stitches and chewing at her loose lower lip. She rocked herself gently.

Stretching an arm into his Drizabone, the old man came back into the room. He walked over to the woman, tapped her arm and said very slowly, 'I'm going out,' and pointed to the door.

She watched him blankly for a moment, then nodded and grunted a string of words I could not understand.

'Yes, I'm going out. I'll be back soon.' He spoke slowly and stroked her arm. 'It's all right,' he said, nodding slowly. He looked at her a moment and then turned to me. 'Better get going. I'll get the truck.'

I let him pass and stood at the door, reluctant to join him in the muddy dash across the yard to the shed. I had only been standing there a few seconds when I felt the woman lumber up behind me. She mumbled something, planted a hand behind my shoulders and pushed me into the rain.

The engine jumped stutteringly to life. We spoke no words as we turned on to the road.

The water had risen a good deal, and now washed against the bottom of the chassis. The old man clucked his tongue and reached under his seat for a chain. 'Wouldn't try to push that,' he said. 'Current's too strong. Bad night, this.' He nudged the truck close to the car and, gathering the chain, ran out into the rain. He gave me no chance to offer help, expressing, I suppose, his contempt of idiots driving out on such a night.

By the truck's headlights I saw his coat flapping wildly behind him as he edged through the water. He lodged a hook around the bumper bar, inched back and hooked the other end to the front of the truck.

'Let's just hope this works,' I said.

He said nothing but 'Water's rising fast,' ground into reverse gear and gunned the engine.

The chain tightened, the car shook and the truck started to skew and slide into the gravel. The car suddenly leaped forward and swung into the line of the pull. He backed away slowly, letting the car roll on to the road.

I went to thank him. He pressed a finger to his mouth and peered out into the night.

'Get in your car and swing it around,' he said.

I was confused as I watched him edge the truck forward so that it rolled into the lapping edge of the water. He yelled at me, vicious against the wind, 'Do as I said, swing your lights around.'

Startled by his anger, I jumped into my car, prayed for a start and brought it around in line. He switched his headlights on to high beam, I did also, and in the light saw some faint white forms clustered ghost-like across the water.

He was rapping at my window. 'Water must've risen in the top paddock and washed them down. You swim?' I blinked with no comprehension. 'Look, there goes a lamb on the mother's back.' He pointed to an indistinct white solid bobbing over the top of the water. And then I heard the high, frail bleat.

'Ever driven at tractor?'

'Once.'

'Good. Follow me back. I'll load the boat on the truck. You bring the tractor and tray.'

There was a flume of gravel as he swung the truck around. For all the return journey I could only follow the flurry of wet grit kicked up in his wake. He dashed across the yard and into the house, opening the door with a slam of the fist. I followed him.

He was bending over the woman. 'Can you do that? Tell Morrie we're at Gordon's Ford. You got that?' He was helping her to her feet and leading her to the telephone. 'Telephone Morrie, Gordon's Ford.' He mouthed the words as she repeated them. 'Good girl. Good.' He turned to me and we left.

I remember little of loading the boat and hooking up the tractor tray. Blessedly, I also recall little of driving the tractor other than being helped up in to the seat and, with his rough hand laid over mine, pushing through the sixteen gears in a quick driving lesson.

I crawled along the road in the wrong gear, falling far behind the fast-disappearing truck and swearing at the rain that I tried to wipe off my face with my elbow.

He had already unloaded the boat and lashed it by a long rope to a tree. He yelled, 'I'm going to lift the ones in the water. There's some stuck on an island but they'll have to stay put a while. Left the back cage and reverse the tray as far as you can into the water and get on it.' Then he turned and, by the light of the torch he held, I saw him start up the stuttering outboard, climb in and cast off. I felt a fear that wasn't my own. He must have been double my age and barely more than half my height.

I wrestled with the cage latch in the darkness, cursing at the coldness of the metal beneath my bare hands. They were now almost locked with numbness. Eventually the latch worked free and the gate swung back heavily. I climbed back on to the tractor and spent time organising the gears into reverse, hoping that the tray would not jack-knife. I did not look behind for I was frightened to think that I might slide too far into the water and never pull out.

I climbed over the wire cage and hung by a numbed hand as close as I dared to the water. The putt-putter of the motor came close. 'Catch the rope and lash it,' he called. Something hit the water near me. I grabbed the end of the rope before it was whipped away in the water. I hauled at it.

'Shit,' he bawled. 'Gently, I nearly fell out then.' He came in close. 'Here, take these.'

Reaching out, I felt a wet fistful of wool. A leg kicked my forearm and I yelled with pain. It had broken the skin and I felt the warmth of my blood rolling over the cold of my skin.

Unsure of the size of it, I stepped back and steadied myself to grab the whole animal. It was a shock, the weight of the struggling wether with its wool soaked with water. Grunting, I grabbed two legs and dragged it backwards on to the tray. I was panting heavily and choking on the rain I had inhaled.

'Good,' said the old man. 'Now the next.'

By the third animal I was gulping air in screaming breaths. The cold air and the wet was searing my lungs, and still I could not breathe deeply enough.

'Hell,' I yelled. 'The tray's sliding into the water.'

'The handbrake, for Chrissakes. Shove the handbrake on.' His voice drifted back over the disappearing stutter of the engine.

I clambered back up the tray, sliding over the sodden forms lying prone and panting. I climbed out of the tray cage and dropped to the ground slumping in a heap where I landed.

By the third haul there was a ribbon of pain across my shoulders and another pulled tightly around my chest. The muscles in my arms were rippled with spasms from the cold and it seemed I could lift them only with a great deal of concentration. And there was the offensive smell of wet, raw wool made more pungent by the scent of urine as the animals pissed themselves at the terror of it all. The warmth of the urine raised steam clouds in the coldness. It smelled like nothing on earth.

The old man had been working constantly by the bare torchlight and against the force of the current. The light aluminium boat would give him no support as he hauled the stock out of the water, using muscles unseen in that spare and stooping frame.

'Just as well they're not in full wool.' His voice came nearer through the darkness.

'Take a break,' I said. 'I'll go out this time.'

There was a silence of indecision and then he said, 'Thanks, if you think you can handle it. I'm fair knackered.'

Emerging into the circle of the headlights, he looked smaller and frailer than I had remembered, the water having plastered his clothes tightly around him. He breathed out great clouds of steam but shook uncontrollably. The hand he rested on mine as I gave him a lift out of the boat was softened by the water and the wool grease. He rested his rangy limbs against the wire cage and sank slowly on to the tray deck.

I cast off the boat and, looking back, saw him lying still among the shifting, steaming bodies of his sheep, a vision cast up in the eerie light and shadow of the car lights. Then the enveloping night closed in as the boat shifted into the current.

Knowing my direction was an imprecise science. The torch threw a fractured line of light across the water, and I saw a large broken limb of a tree spike past in the current. The sides of the light boat suddenly seemed very thin, and the fear in me became very real.

The head of a sheep appeared out of the water near by. I choked the motor down to a gurgle and crawled to the bow. The boat rocked drunkenly as I reached over to grab the animal. With the other hand I reached between the flailing legs and tried to haul it in.

Holding the sheep in an embrace of mutual terror. I felt the boat dipping dangerously. I could see its terrified face, its yellow eyes wild and staring. I tried to get a stronger grip, bracing myself further back in the boat to correct the lean. It kicked still more and, upsetting my balance, pulled me over towards the side. There was water washing up into the boat. I panicked, sprang open my arms and fell back. The animal slipped away into the dark, its final cries soon lost in the roar of water and wind.

For some time I just lay crumpled in the bow of the boat, feeling defeated as I had never felt.

Out of the night came another animal, a lamb floating on the bloated body of a ewe. It bleated its distress high and piteously and I could not help but reach out, lift it up and bring it lightly aboard. It was simple. I looked for more lambs, arguing with myself that younger stock were more worth saving. Before long I had another and the boat was holding more stable.

Back on the road, I could see more headlights flashing up

and I realised that Morrie must have arrived. Heartened, I caught hold of a ewe as it swept past and, holding it in close embrace, hauled it quickly over the side and into the boat. There was elation singing in me as I rolled it to the bow. It lay silent a while. The bastard was dead. I grabbed the head in my hands. Its open glassy eyes started at me mutely, its monstrous silly tongue lolling. 'Shit you, shit you.' I was pounding the carcass with my fist. I stood up and kicked it. In fury I rolled it back over the side, watching with satisfaction as it hit the water and washed away. I kicked up the motor and started back, wishing no more than to hand up the lambs and get away from all this.

The old man was sitting inside the truck cabin, slowly sipping a mug of tea, when I found him. Morrie and his sons had come equipped not only with another boat and more lights but also with a flask of hot, sweet, black tea. It burned a passage down me and I have never tasted better.

The others were pulling the last stragglers into the tray. We counted more than thirty animals and the old man guessed as many had been lost. He seemed satisfied.

Sometimes there was something said, more often it was a nod where none had been before. Soon after the sheep rescue at Gordon's Ford I received the first of several congratulations from people I couldn't really say I knew. One night a beer appeared over the bar and Molloy jerked his head towards the other end of the room where a fellow lifted his glass in an anonymous toast. It was not an unpleasant time.

Pat must have heard, too, and to show his approval he warned me away from a consideration that would have otherwise cost me dear. 'They'll have to go hunting that one with a hurricane lamp,' he warned. But he cleaned me up in the next race – a man's admiration can only go so far.

'About eight inches on a good day,' he added.

I was thumbing through a pile of cattle-market reports when he slid into my office. 'How did you find the old lady out there?' He asked the question with his eyes fixed on the wall behind me.

'A bit odd. Not all there.'

He sat on the edge of my desk, facing away from me and rubbing the inside of his calf muscle.

'She slammed the door on me at first. The husband had to let me in. She just acted as though I wasn't there, and when he spoke to her it was like he was talking to a child. Odd. You know them?'

'Sort of.'

'Well?'

'No, no. I don't know them all that well. Not them. Not now. Haven't seen them in a good while, a good while.' He kept rubbing his leg. 'But I remember the stories about her, the nicest looker hereabouts, they used to say. They all said he'd made a killing when he'd married her – ooh, bit wedding, too. A killing and a bad mistake. Some women are pretty and they don't know it. Others are just pretty and they do. And if a man's got something between his ears as well as something between his legs, he knows which is which. This bloke didn't, and couldn't get over why all the seed salesmen and fencing contractors kept calling in. Got his wind up proper, it did. He used to chase them off with the wrong end of a shotgun. Well, things happened and she was in the club but when the tiddler came she fell sick. Very sick she was. She was having the baby at home and something went wrong. The kid died and she spent weeks having fits and turns. But the old man wouldn't take her to hospital – he said it was just her mourning for the lost kid – but everyone said it was because he was too stingy, that he wouldn't bring in a doctor because of what it might cost him.'

He leaned in closer. 'What it really was,' – he paused – 'was that he didn't see why he should pay for a kid that wasn't his. He'd done a bit of reckoning and figured that she must have lifted her skirts in another direction. Cuckolded like a Jacobean husband. It got his goat and he just sat tight. She pulled out of the fever eventually, but it had done something to her brain – curdled it. And he's put up with it ever since. Hasn't told a soul, but I know. That's the reason she's like that and that's the reason he's like that – still thinks it was someone else's kid.'

'And was it?'

'Could be,' he said, and a sadder, slower smile I've yet to see on the face of a man.

He Who Would Valiant Be

It seemed one of life's great mysteries when I looked up from my Saturday paper to see the thin, excited figure of Father Ellis scurrying across the yard to the front door. He bent over, bracing himself against the winds that whipped up over the plains, and hurried towards the house. I could think of no likely explanation for his visit.

St Michael's was the solemn stand of bluestone set back from the road on the outskirts of town. It must have dated back to the start of the century, and was doubtless built with public subscriptions from the faithful flock. It cast around itself a mantle of sobriety, and duty, and represented that day of the week when these qualities were considered virtues.

As its priest, Father Ellis had the task of ministry to the town, but he always freely acknowledged that the scope of his influence was limited to a handful of widows attentive to the life hereafter. It was a faithful flock, but an old one, and prone to death. He tended to take that personally. But he tried, that myopic little man fuelled with nervous energy and blighted with a lisp. He was a regular visitor to the newspaper office, bringing information about church services and youth fellowship outings, and he seemed a dedicated, and long-suffering soldier of the Cross.

'Good morning, Father. Come in.'

'Thank you, Thank you. Foul wind.'

'Yes. Looks like rain could be following up soon.'

'Indeed,' he said, shouldering off his coat and searching for somewhere to hang it. 'Still, rain wouldn't be amiss.'

'You're right, Father. Would you like to sit down in the lounge-room?'

'No, no. I'm fine.' He seemed more excited than usual. He flustered around with his coat and sounded breathless.

'Would you like a cup of coffee?'

'Oh, yes, yes. Tea please. If you have it. If it isn't too much trouble. Thank you.'

'White?'

'Tea. What? Oh, yes, please, Tea with milk, please. And sugar too, please. If you have it.'

He followed me into the kitchen and perched on the edge of the table. He wetted a finger and stabbed at the scattered breadcrumbs. Samovar watched him archly for a moment and stole away.

'Are you well?' he asked.

'Fine. One sugar?'

'Two.'

Tam's voice drifted down the hall. 'Damn it, Samovar, stop humping my slippers. Perverted cat.'

I couldn't shut the door in time. 'We've company here, Tam,' I yelled.

'Who's calling at this goddamned time of the morning?'

'The vicar,' I called back, waiting for the silence.

There was a short silence. 'Who?'

Father Ellis jumped up and started down the hall, calling as he went, 'Father Ellis from St Michael's.' He put his head around the door and then pulled it back again. I imagined the naked body of Tam sprawled across the bed with a bottle frozen to his lips.

Father Ellis beetled back to the kitchen. 'I think your housemate could be suffering from the excesses of the previous night.'

'Highly likely.'

'You know, it's sad really.' He lowered his voice and kept an eye on the door. 'It's sad when people haven't got something fulfilling to do with their time. Like our young men's fellowship. It meets every Thursday night. They have a very interesting social programme too, you know. They organise things. They run the raffle at the annual church fête. Do you think your friend . . . ?'

'Probably not.'

'Ah well.' He sipped his tea thoughtfully. 'It's very hard you know. Very hard indeed.'

He stroked his throat and cast his eyes around the ceiling. 'I try to encourage pastoral activities, groups and that sort of thing. I think it's the role of the modern Church, to get involved in the community.' He took another sip. 'But it's very hard. There are so many other diversions. Yes... very hard.'

'Tea all right?'

'Fine, fine. Now, some of our groups are going very nicely. The young wives' club, that's very active. They raise money for the overseas missions. And they cook and... and embroider things. Marvellous what women can do these days. Do you have any biscuits?'

'Sorry.'

'No matter. And the church choir. Very enthusiastic they are, very. Although they do need some direction. They're very dedicated but... oh dear, how can one say it? They do need a helping hand. They just need a little musical guidance, I suppose.' He was staring deeply into his cup. 'I believe you're quite musical?'

'Not really.'

'But you can read music?'

'Well, yes. In a fashion.'

'And you play?'

'Just my old guitar.'

Father Ellis nodded and started stirring his tea. 'Your editor is very musical too. Well, he appreciates good music.'

'Oh yes?' I had always considered Hegarty a man intolerant of frippery.

'Oh yes. Mr Hegarty is a regular parishioner. Every Sunday you know. His wife makes him, of course. Most of them do. But he's a very important parishioner. And charming. And influential – if you understand?'

I understood.

'And a man of culture. A man who appreciates good music – like yourself.'

I gave an uncertain nod.

'Just the other week I was talking to him about this. Last Saturday I think it was. I was talking to him about the choir business, about their enthusiasm, about their talent – which is quite considerable actually. And that's unusual for a place like this, you must agree?'

I had to agree.

'And I was saying to him how they needed direction. They

just haven't the musical expertise. And he suggested that you might have something to offer. Just a little something to lift their ... their ... musicality.'

'I really don't think ...'

'Oh, he seemed quite certain that you had the ability. And it's only an hour rehearsal once a week. Tuesdays, six p.m. See I've written down the details for you on this piece of paper,' he said pushing it into my hand.

'It's just that my work makes it difficult for me to fit in regular schedules. Deadlines, meetings, more meetings.' I had used this excuse so often before, I was starting to sound convincing.

'Mr Hegarty said he could arrange for you to have those nights off. He was going to talk to you himself but I thought I might just pop in today ... Since I was going past.' He sipped his tea and watched the next drip from the tap hit the unwashed dishes in the sink. 'And he really is a most charming man.'

'And influential.'

'And that, yes.'

He straightened himself, looking a good deal more relieved and relaxed. 'That was an excellent cup of tea. But I've got so many other houses to visit. I like to make the rounds of the parish every so often, just to keep in touch, you know. So many houses to visit, so many cups of tea to drink. At least it flushes out my system.'

'Yes.'

'Well, I suppose I'll be seeing you soon. Tuesday in fact.' He gathered his coat and wrestled with it. 'Oh yes – if your friend would like to join the fellowship ... you might like to mention it. You never know.'

'You never do.'

'Good, good.' He seemed genuinely pleased. And so he might. I once landed a four-pound bream with a tough old piece of leather tied to the hook. I knew the feeling.

Tam waited for the departing sound of the car before he wandered out into the kitchen, scratching himself and looking fazed. 'What was that?'

'Just God moving in mysterious ways. He made me an offer I couldn't refuse. I daren't refuse. I'n the new choir-leader at the church.'

'What?'

'You mean pardon.'

'What?'

'Choir-leader.'

'You mean little boys? Pre-pubescent little boys? Fair-skinned little cherubs untouched and untried?'

'Lay off.'

'And little girls? All ripe for . . . ?'

'Plug it, Tam.'

'Not to mention the good matrons. They don't tell, they don't swell and they're as grateful as hell.'

'Leave off.'

'Wassamadda? Did de big, bad priestums scare little diddums?'

'Leave off.'

'All right. All right, songbird.' He wandered back into his room, calling back, 'I didn't know they fitted Sherman tanks with dog-collars.' And some minutes later, 'Oh, my God. Choir-leader. Holy Howitzer.' And he was still giggling over it that afternoon.

Cold as a cavern and full of echo, St Michael's church hall didn't look half as inviting as Molloy's that Tuesday night. The huddle of choristers stamped their feet against the chill and blew on their fingers while the voice of Father Ellis soared up and away in unbridled flight.

' . . . saved the world's cultural heritage in the darkest days of heathenism. For while the Dark Ages descended, bringing the afflictions of pestilence, disease and misery, the tradition of sacred music preserved and embodied the highest of humanity's exiled ideals. This,' – he paused dramatically – 'this is your noble heritage. And this' – he swung an arm out to me – 'this is the man to help you.'

The choir turned in a single action and regarded me stonily. Most of them were dumpy women with a scattering of girls and a lone, pale youth with painfully prominent buck-teeth. Father Ellis started clapping and they followed limply.

He grabbed my elbow, not smiling but waving an arm towards the group. 'Let me introduce you to Mrs Frith, Mrs Ford, Mrs Travers, Gillian Warrington, Narlene Printz – ' He spoke in a quick-fire rat-tat-tat. There was a flash of faces before me. 'Marie . . . Marie Couch? Crouch. Marie Crouch, Mrs Unger, Mrs Hall, her son, Thomas, Miss Williams, Karen, Kirin and

Kerryn Matthews; Merryn and Erin Daniels, and Mrs Vaughan, our pianist.'

Seated at the piano, Mrs Vaughan scowled. She had all the personal allure of a fully laden lorry, and shared much the same dimensions.

'Mrs Vaughan had had the responsibility of this choir for quite a few years,' said Father Ellis, pulling the pin from the grenade.

'Fourteen years,' She drew herself up on her piano stool. 'Fourteen years I have led this choir and . . .'

' . . . and a very good job she had done of it too,' said Father Ellis. 'She has achieved a great deal in this time. A great deal.' He was furiously scratching his palm. 'Perhaps we could show you just a small sample of what she has taught them. Do you think we could do that, Mrs Vaughan?'

She released a long, pained sigh, and struck up a pompous and ponderous introduction to 'Jerusalem', with not a few wrong notes. The choir joined in raggedly, barely keeping rhythm or tune. Facing them, I could do nothing but keep a wan smile plastered across my face. When they finished the first verse, they stood silent, awaiting my verdict.

'A very . . . very distinctive tone you have there,' I offered.

'It is, of course, our showpiece,' said Mrs Vaughan.

'Of course.'

'And there is a great deal more that they can do.'

'Indeed there is,' chipped in Father Ellis, now rubbing the inside of his wrist with vigour. 'All they need is a little polishing. They just need some rounding off. That's all really. A bit of scrub up. A bit of a brush down. That's all.' He must have removed three layers of skin by that time.

'And so, what do you intend to do?' Mrs Vaughan spoke from deep within her sizeable mass.

'Well.' I took a long breath. 'Perhaps we could just start with a little revision. Just to cover the things you already know. Just to . . . go over them, sort of.' The air had leaked out of me.

'Such as,' Mrs Vaughan was clearly on the hunt.

'Basic things. Notes, for instance.' I avoided her glare and swung away to face the choir with a look of what must have been sheer terror. 'Let me hear you all sing this note.' I started, and gradually their voices joined mine. I tried them up the scale and down. Up again and down.

'Good, good,' I lied. 'Now, let's hear the sopranos do that scale.' There was silence. 'Sopranos. Do you have any sopranos?'

'We've never bothered with that side of it,' said Mrs Vaughan, her voice as threatening as the wrong end of a cannon.

'And quite rightly,' I quickly added, fearing a spark would touch the gunpowder within. 'We don't want peripheries getting in the way of the music, do we.' I was talking quickly and sweating wildly. 'But perhaps it would be interesting just to define our sections, don't you think?'

'We've never done it before,' said Big Bertha at the keyboard.

'But just as an experiment . . . ?' Sugar was dripping from the edge of my voice.

'Please, Mrs Vaughan. Just an experiment,' echoed Father Ellis.

She turned wordlessly back to her piano.

I sighed audibly. 'Now, ladies. If you could please sing up the scale with me, one by one. The lady on the end, Mrs . . . er . . .'

'Ford,' said Father Ellis.

'Frith,' said Mrs Frith.

She joined me on the upwards path, singing straight down her nose and straining at the top notes. 'Keep going, Mrs Frith,' I urged. She wavered and cracked, sitting down flushed from the exertion and the embarrassment. 'I think perhaps you are an alto, Mrs Frith,' I said, trying to keep the brightness in my voice. 'That means you sing the lovely rich lower bits.' She blinked and looked away. A long murmur swept through the rest of the group.

'Now, perhaps that little girl behind you. Er, Kerryn?'

'Kirin,' said Father Ellis.

'Karen,' she whispered. Her voice as a breath of noise that barely brushed the air.

'Perhaps you could do with some help from the girl beside you,' I suggested. 'Kerryn?'

'Merryn,' said Father Ellis.

'Erin,' the child said, before dissolving into a fit of giggles that spread through the rest of the girls. They cackled and squawked like scattered hens, and Father Ellis slapped his arms and crowed above the din, 'Children, children. Quiet please!' Mrs Vaughan, who had been watching fixedly, turned to her piano and thumped a chord loudly. A hush fell quickly over the group, and eyes were averted.

'Perhaps we could now start the practice.' Each of her words weighed heavily in the silence. 'If you've finished your experiment?'

I could only nod.

'Good,' she said.

Father Ellis sought to apply a salve. 'Perhaps you could conduct while Mrs Vaughan played,' he suggested.

'I am perfectly capable of both tasks, Father Ellis,' said Mrs Vaughan. 'For fourteen years I have both accompanied and conducted this choir.'

'It would just mean that you could concentrate more on the accompaniment,' said Father Ellis, losing his grip.

'Are you suggesting my piano-playing has been less than satisfactory until now?' She was tightening hers.

'No, no...'

'Are you suggesting that I am not a capable pianist?'

'It's just that...' I caught back my words – too late.

'And who are you?' She whirled around, glowering at me. 'Just who are you? Some trumped-up something dragged in here.'

'Well, look, I really didn't want to...'

'And it shows. Look what you've done here tonight. You've made this rehearsal a circus. We were managing very nicely before you came along. You... you impostor!'

'Nicely? Managing nicely?' I felt my voice rise. 'This bunch were bellowing like de-nutted tomcats.'

She caught her breath and then exploded. 'Insolence!'

'And since you ask, I very strongly suspect your abilities as a pianist.' I could hear Father Ellis making tutting noises round my left ear.

'Liar!'
'Incompetent!'
'Usurper!'
'Philistine!'
'Heathen!'
'Fraud!'

'Communist!' She jumped to her feet, the mass of her torso wobbling behind her. 'Father, I resign!'

It was all around town by the morning. Hegarty was delighted, proving himself to be more of a music-lover than I had ever imagined.

Loser Takes All

The word soon got out that Fate had chosen one of the locals to scoop the top prize in a major lottery. So large was the win that the recipient had insisted the lottery company withhold their name, fearing its release would result in a steady trail of beggars to their door.

I began my hunt at Molloy's. 'Yes. I heard about that too,' said Mick, pulling another glass. 'Whoever it is, I wish to hell they'd come and celebrate it here.' Then he yelled, 'Any of you mob know who won that lottery?'

'I did,' came a voice from the crowd.

'You lying bugger. I did,' came another.

A lifetime in a small country town does strange things to a man's sense of humour.

'You're both liars,' said another. 'I won it, but I've gone and drunk it all.'

'Anyway,' said Mick. 'What would you do with it? A million dollars? More trouble than it's worth.'

'You're right there,' said Morrie.

'You could pay off that outpaddock you bought last year, Morrie. You know, the one you bought to grow thistles,' said Peter Spratt.

'Go bite your bum. Mind you, I could always do with a new combine harvester,' Morrie said.

'No, my missus would spend it all. I wouldn't see a scarp of it.'

'She'd buy herself a new husband.'

'And I wouldn't stop her.'

'I think I'd sell up and go north,' said Pete Maguire. 'Good beef country up there.'

'I know what I'd do. I'd buy a pub, lock the door and die.'

I continued the hunt and called in to see old man Parker. He tried to sell me some trouser buttons. 'Gambling contravenes God's holy laws,' he said. 'Buy some of these instead. You never know when you'll need them.'

I tried old man Tilson and all the Printz boys. I even asked Nigs. 'Mere bread and circuses for the plebs,' he said, wielding a monkey wrench as if it were a nail file. 'Faint hopes and vain glories while the lottery company bosses rake in the real fortunes.'

Pat had not received any large plunges from any of his customers, but suggested, 'How's about asking the newsagent? He would have sold the winning ticket.'

'No idea,' said the newsagent, busy stocking his shelves. 'Sell thousands of tickets each week. Could have been any of them.'

'But don't you get notified about any major winners?' I asked.

'Yes, but not the name,' he said. 'And if it's for the *Weekly Ad.*, I wouldn't tell you anyway. I've got work to get done. If you ask me, your paper's only fit to line the bottom of the budgie's cage. And you can tell that to Hegarty too, if you like.'

It was the first and the last time I ever exchanged words with him. The following week he took sick and by the Friday he was dead. A brain tumour, they discovered, which had been lurking for many years, had suddenly flared and snuffed him out.

His memory was hailed in a few sessions at Molloy's front bar – but not that many. It seemed he had possessed more than just a knack of rubbing people up the wrong way, and it was decided among the drinkers that his brain must have been turning sour for years before.

It was while I was attending one of the wakes that Pam edged up to me with an air of the conspirator about her. 'You know how you were asking about the lottery winner?'

'Yes.'

'Well, I was having my hair done the other day. Mrs Maguire as lives out beyond the school used to be a hairdresser and now she does home visits. And she was telling me that one of the Templeton kids had told her son that his family were the ones that won that big prize.'

'The Templetons?'

'I know. Can you believe it?' she said. 'Still, it could go to worse places. At least they'll be able to use it, not stick it in the bank and live like fat cats on the hearth-rug. It's a good thing, I say. They may have their faults, those people. But I'm glad the money's gone to them.'

'You're probably right.' I drained my glass. 'Thanks, Pam, you're a real treat. Here, have one on me. I'll be seeing you.'

Everyone knew something about the Templetons. They had a gaggle of children spanning a wide range of ages, and to feed them all the father, Bill, took up occasional farm-hand work whenever the chance arose. They lived as far out as possible in the red country, where the land was cheap but the soil was heartbreakingly poor. More than once the stock agents had advised Bill Templeton to sell up and pull out, but he refused with the vigour of a man committed to a life task and to spite their warnings he somehow managed to limp on through a succession of bad seasons.

His cattle were scrawny and wild-eyed, much like the children he raised. A group of them together looked like a handful of fire-blackened twigs, and it was said there could be a bit of aborigine in some of them. Bill Templeton was a bit short on brain cells – all his family were. With the remoteness of their farm and the shift of the sand dunes blocking the roads to it, the gossips of the town hinted at some family liaisons that defied biblical law.

'What's the definition of confusion?' the jibe went. 'Father's Day at the Templetons'.'

Sometimes the children attended school, shuffling around in their ill-fitting shoes – when they wore any shoes at all – and in their ragbag of castaway clothes provided by charity. Their noses dripped incessantly and they made great show of wiping them on the backs of their sleeves. One of the boys was deaf, another had bad vision and they all had thick blubbery mouths that revealed very few teeth. Schoolyard bullies made them regular prey when they turned up for lessons. The remoteness of their home made things impossible for the truant inspectors when they didn't.

Martha knew where it was, and drew a map of indistinct distances and uncertain directions for me. She called the children 'a bunch of magpies' and told me to lock away any valuables I had in the car. 'They may be millionaires, but they're still magpies,' she warned.

Driving past the town limits, I made a quick check of the

petrol gauge. The water was fine, and the oil also. The journey out there I figured would take the best part of an hour, and possibly more, so imprecise were the directions I had received. The difficulty lay in distinguishing the landmarks for a track, a tank or a waterhole standing out from the endless sameness of the dunes, and there was no guarantee that they hadn't since been covered over and lost to sight. The road itself may have disappeared under the spread of sand.

The first ten miles I covered easily, for the road skirted the edges of Lake Eummerang, a large, shallow lake that quickly evaporated into a salt pan in the early summer. But now it was still holding water, and was a beautiful sight. There was a scattering of twisted mallee growing along the fringe and a mixture of hardy native grasses across the ground. The water lay flat and calm as death, reflecting the clear blue of the sky and adding to it its own soft glitter. Already the level had started to subside, revealing the rich terracotta mud beneath. The mud that backed to brick-hardness in the summer was still oozing and alive with the insects that drew the wading birds from hundreds of miles away. Lanky ibis and spoonbill dotted the lake, casting their small black reflections. I knew they were the last living things I would see in the stretch ahead to the Templetons', and they rested easily on my eyes. If I had have been an artist I would come here more often.

Beyond the lake the road struck off to the west and trailed a lonely path between the rise and fall of the dunes. I kept an eye open for the landmarks on Martha's map, found them, and felt happy.

The dunes appeared to follow a regular pattern of deposition. The early afternoon sun barely cast a shadow on them, but against the flat red colour I could pick out the fine blues and purples cast up by the ripples in the sands. A patch of salt bush broke the line of the dunes. and then a scattering of marram, toughened and bleached almost white by the sun.

From time to time a small track wound off from the road, and I was curious as to where it led. I wondered how long it had been since anybody had gone into the red country beyond the road, and indeed if anyone had ever done so since the aborigines roamed the land. It seemed to be country timeless, yet full of time.

Then it began to flatten out. The horizon sat as a straighter line and more distant. There was no sign of a power pole or a telephone line. I supposed the Templetons had lived long enough without technology to bother. But as I considered this, I heard a faint clatter far off across the red stretches. A generator perhaps, I thought, or a pump motor. Driving closer, I saw the tiny shape of the pump head to an Artesian bore, its fan-like sails standing still in the air. Drawing closer still, I saw a man climbing around the metal frame.

'Morning,' I said to the lanky youth wrapped around the fretwork. 'I'm looking for the Templeton place.'

He looked at me silently, his expression flat and unblinking.

I spoke louder. 'I'm looking for the Templeton place. Do you know where it is?'

He raised an arm and pointed down the road.

'Thank you,' I nodded energetically. 'Are you a Templeton?'

He made no response.

Obviously not big on conversation these people.

Fences appeared along the roadside – ancient wooden post and barbed wire boundaries that tottered and twisted in bad need of repair. I saw, on the left, a cluster of buildings and a collection of vehicles, so I turned down the track towards them. Panicking chickens scattered before my car. They were all red with dust. A scrawny old dog reluctantly climbed to its feet and wandered over with an air of indifference. A scrabble of cats stalked away and hid in the shade of a shed, watching all the while with narrowed eyes as I stopped in the yard in front of the house.

The dog made a slow and thorough study of the car, sniffing it archly all the way around, and holding a pose that reminded me of a shadow-boxer. Then he cocked a leg against a wheel, piddled a little and slunk away.

The farm buildings around the yard were unimpressive. Thrown together with building scraps and rough handiwork, they buckled and leaned awkwardly. The unseasoned eucalyptus trunks used for uprights had warped with time, peeling away from the sheets of galvanised iron and finally sagging so that they lay almost parallel to the earth. Derelict cars and trucks littered the yard, many with their automotive innards spilled out and scattered. Rusted and deserted farm machinery lay discarded in the red dust, and the remains of household rubbish were left to languish unburnt and uncovered for the swarms of bushflies. A bony old stock horse in a paddock shook itself, releasing a cloud of red dust from its coat.

They had doubtless seen me arrive, but the Templetons offered no welcoming party. I walked up to the house across the wide, unshaded expanse of sand. The building has presumably once been a house. There could have been panes of glass in the empty window frames and a door that hung properly, instead of dangling from one hinge. The debris of the yard piled up on to the verandah: a saddle pulled apart, a child's bicycle without handlebars or wheels, a couple of empty fruit cans and more than a couple of empty beer cans.

'Hello?' I called. 'Anyone there?'

'What do you want?' There was a woman as thin and bony as everything else about the place standing behind me in the yard. She wore a faded flowered apron that flapped loosely around her calves, and on one hip she balanced a baby wearing only a grubby singlet.

'Mrs Templeton?' I started walking across the yard. She backed away.

'What do you want?' She had a tic that put one side of her face into spasms. Her face was drawn and hollowed-out and she had the tight lips and fixed scowl that all women assume in the glare and heat of these parts. She had once been a handsome woman, with fine dark eyes, but had since dried up to bitterness.

I introduced myself.

'You'll want to speak to my husband then,' she said, backing further away.

'I'll speak to you.'

'No, you'll want to speak to my husband. Bill? Bill?' she bawled out across the yard. 'Bill?'

A man appeared from the shed and started walking towards us. He walked with a short-legged roll, like that of a man too long on horseback. As he walked he wiped his hands on an oily cloth, but he did not shake my hand. He had the same tight set to his face. He was as rough and brown as old leather. A couple of tall lads emerged from a shed and sauntered up behind him. They were as wiry and tanned as their father.

'Yes?' he said.

'I'm from the *Weekly Ad.*,' I started.

'Yes.'

'And I'm following up some news from town that the big lottery has been won locally.'

'And?'

'The talk around town is that you may be the winner.'

'Yes?'

The two boys started murmuring to each other, their hands shielding their mouths. A flock of girls emptied out of the house on to the verandah and stood there giggling. They had their hands pushed deeply into the pockets of their shapeless dresses. They were all lean, and several of the younger ones balanced on one leg like a gathering of flamingos.

'Get inside, you lot,' the woman called. 'Go on, get.' A toddler with a dribbling nose wandered up to her and grabbed the trailing hem of her dress.

'Is it true?'

'What?'

'The lottery win.'

'Well . . .' He scuffed at the dirt with the side of his boot. 'Don't know about that now.'

The toddler tumbled over into the sand and sat there picking up tiny handfuls and throwing them at my legs.

'You'd surely know if you'd won a million dollars,' I said.

'How much?'

'A million dollars.'

He turned to the woman and then to the youths. They all wore blank faces.

'Dunno,' he said, pulling a piece of cotton thread from his sleeve and drawing it through his teeth.

'You don't know if you've won?'

'We don't get to hear all that much out here,' he said.

'But they must have sent you a telegram, a letter?'

'No once much writes to us. Only bills.'

An older man, one with a walk like a hiccup, came up to us.

'Hey, Dad. This bloke here reckons we've won a million dollars,' Bill said.

'Yes?' The old man had a throat filled with rust, 'That's nice.'

'Look, it's only what people are saying,' I interrupted. 'And I just called to check . . .'

'A million,' said the old man. 'We could buy a new bull with that, Bill.'

'Dunno, Dad. I'd rather get a new distributor for the truck. Saw one the other day in the scrap yard at Wirralla. It'd need a bit of doing up, though.'

'But you haven't heard officially that you've won this money?' I tried to squeeze into the conversation.

'We could go into sheep, Bill,' said the old man. 'This'd be good sheep country.'

'You're not wrong there, Dad. There's a lot of money in sheep these days.'

'Hang on. You may not have even won the money,' I said. It was too late.

'We'd have to put up a woolshed. I suppose we could knock together a shearing shed. We could butt it up behind the hayshed,' said Bill, wandering off in thought.

'There'd be shearing gear you'd be needing too, Bill. You'd have to buy that, remember,' his wife said, trailing behind him.

'Do you think we could do anything with the old stock yards?' said the old man. 'Let's have a look at those too while we're out there.'

I watched them walk away.

'How much do you reckon a shearing team'd cost?'

'We could always bring the kids in to help.'

'Yeh. That'd keep down the cost.'

They wandered off across the yard, oblivious of me, intent only on their new-born project. I sighed, climbed into the car and drove off. Daydreams, after all, cost nothing and don't depend on the luck of the draw.

About thirty miles out from town I passed Sergeant Lawson speeding along the road. He braked sharply when he saw me and pulled up alongside.

'You all right?' he asked.

'Yes, thanks. Why?'

'Heard you were going out to the Templetons'.'

'Yes.'

'And you're all right?'

'Yes. Fine. No problems out there. They're just a little backward, that's all.'

'Yes, well.' He flicked some fluff off his trousers. 'Just checking. It's a long drive out there and you could get lost or bogged in the sand. Most people just pop into the police station to tell us before they head off out into the red country. Just in case, you know. Bloke died out there about five years ago. His car stalled in the heat. Died from thirst in three days.'

'Fair enough. Sorry to cause any trouble,' I said. 'I'll remember that next time.'

'Good,' he said, turning back to his car. 'It's all right, I wasn't too busy anyway. Only had one thing to do all morning – witness the death certificate signing.'

'The newsagent?'

'Yes. You'd never believe it. His wife told me he was the poor bastard that went and won all that money on the lottery. The richest stiff in town.' He erupted into a wheezing laugh. 'Cut me off at the legs and call me Shorty. I could hardly stop myself laughing.'

Bloody Waste

The summer had been dragging on with a heat to knock a man senseless. The spring rains had trailed off early and the drought had begun before Christmas. Now, seven weeks later, it looked like a fifth of the wheat crop was lost. The sheep cull had started and droves of cattle wandering the roadsides for feed were becoming a familiar sight. Things could only get worse, they said.

Each day the plum-voiced sound of the radio announcer sang out the drought's litany: the noon report of the dropping river levels. The smaller waterways were now dry scars carved through the land, and once-mighty rivers moving slowly and broadly had withered into muddy brooks, their beds parched and scattered over with stones. Nature all-bountiful had turned against the farmers and there was not a man who could change that.

Drought ages a landscape. It sucks dry the waterholes and etches a network of cracks through the drying mud of the dams. Cattle struggling to suck out the dregs of moisture coughed on the congealed mud and – later, as it dried further – licked at the hard-baked surface in animal ignorance.

Farmers were trucking in water and trucking in feed – paying dearly for both and knowing no way to pay.

The cracks in the earth widened and spread, leaving well-tended paddocks wizened. The earth looked as wild and inhospitable as the moon. Grass that turned yellow in the heat finally dried out completely and, losing its dying grip on the soil, bundled and tumbled away in the hot winds driving in from the north.

Stripped of cover, the soil became restless. Whipping up and away in red flurries, it bit at the legs of men and stock. It stung at the skin and embittered the heart. The thin, rich layer of topsoil was escaping the drought that the farmers had to endure. They could only stand and watch as their most precious asset whirled up high into the sky and sped away to the coast.

The crops they had planted simply could not germinate in the brick-hard earth. The stock were dying and more were being culled, shot and dumped into big pits that were becoming a more common sight at the crossroads. They chose the weakest animals and the least profitable. The sheep that lay panting, unable to raise their heads, were hauled into trucks and taken to the pits for shooting. The cattle, licking each other's hides for sweat or lying with their tongues lolling in the dust, were shot and bulldozed into the quickly filling holes. In all the hot haze kicked up around the pits, the stiffened limbs of the animals struck a grotesque silhouette at each day's end.

Stud breeders had a desperate hunt for agistment for their valuable animals in the greener parts of the country. Politicians said many things, even those hailing from the sewered suburban blocks. Prayers for rain came from pulpits, banks beefed up rural loans and trucking companies ran hot with work.

Farmers, meanwhile, set to their daily task of shooting and dumping. They worked together, grim and silent under the big, red sky. I watched them working in a sweat of frustration, as though they were participating in some type of purge. Dust-caked and spattered with blood, they worked until they were drained and there was no light left in the day. And when they went home it was to sleep the sleep of sad men.

The office, at least, was cool inside its walls, and Molloy's was even more so. I did not venture far from either during the day. An advantage of the heat was that as soon as you poured a beer into you, it immediately vaporised into sweat, allowing you to down more glasses than normal.

Increased drinking, coupled with the monotony of the heat, meant that I sank into a period of listlessness. The main cause, however, was insomnia. It was too hot to lie under sheets and blankets, but not to be covered at night meant you were easy prey for the mosquitoes that bred in the water-tanks and bore-holes of the area. They were monsters of insects, big-bellied and hungry as a pack of hounds. They were equipped with some unearthly sense of knowing where to find a likely victim even in the dark. I read it was something to do with differing air pressures brought on by breathing – and I could not stop breathing in my sleep. It was also said that they could be attracted by the scent of human sweat. Trying to stop that in this heat was just as impossible. You could not shut them out. You could kill a score and still find more clinging to the ceiling. They thrived on insect spray and paid callous disregard to smoke-repellent coils.

At night, lying half-sensible from fatigue, I would lie listening for the high-pitched whine of their wings. Tense, uncertain and strung-out, I felt like a Londoner in the Blitz, waiting helplessly for the approach of the enemy. And when the sound came I would jump for the light, swinging out madly with the sole of my slipper at anything airborne. If I scored a hit, they squashed against the wall, exploding with their nightly harvest of blood. I relished the distastefulness of it all.

Sometimes I woke Tam with my attacks and curses. I bould hear him chuckle, being one of those blessed people that even mosquitoes won't go near.

I wanted sympathy, and Pat agreed to put up with my bleating for a while.

'You really shouldn't complain,' he said, finally.
'But damn it, Pat, I need my sleep.'
'Don't we all?'
'I must have been awake for sixty hours now.'
'Then you're a lucky man. We all have the heat and we all have the mosquitoes, but not all of us live near the meatworks,' he said.

And he was right. People down-wind of the plant tolerated the stench most of the time. Its warm, hot stink sometimes blew into town on an eastern wind and made everyone bilious. The main culprit was the rendering plant where fat and offal was stewed into an evil mass that came out as deceptively excellent fertiliser.

'If it's not the stink from the rendering plant, it's the pong of the live animals,' he said. 'They're all penned up tight, shitting and pissing and making a hell of a racket. Dante would feel right at home there.'

My case had lost its clout.

He continued. 'And now it's worse. Everyone's culling their herds for the drought. It should be full production up there.'

'You're right, you're right.'

'But it won't get any better. Not with some of the meatworkers going out.'

'What's this?' I asked.

'Some of the blokes are going on strike, reckon they need more staff and more money for all the extra work they're doing with the culling,' he said. 'I think the boning-room boys went out last week. And I know the beef-chain men are thinking of joining them. It's madness. A bit like this place on press day.'

'So what's happening to the stock?'

'Well, with the handlers out on strike they'll only be able to slaughter and chuck the carcasses out for dog food. Mightn't even be able to get the skins. Still, the culling means the market's so flooded the price won't be high enough to worry the farmers.'

'And if all the blokes go out?'

'The stock are stuck there to rot.'

'But couldn't they take them to another meatworks?'

'You've got to be kidding. The way the prices are falling it's not worth the cost trucking them any great distance. Besides, there's rumbles at all the other works too. They're all under pressure. Even the Nooweep knackery,' said Pat. 'Unless some promising nags make a showing on the racetrack soon they'll be filling Fido's bowl. Bloody sad.'

'So what are the farmers doing?'

'Well, some of them'll start shooting stock on their properties. Others will just keep shipping them in here and they'll pack in the animals tighter and tighter until the strike is on proper. And then they'll leave the stock in the holding pens and enough of them'll die and the farmers will sue for compensation from the meatworks and the meatworks will claim government subsidy to repay that cost and everyone will be happy. Usually happens that way.'

'I think there's a story in this, Pat.'

'You be careful. Those men are dab hands with long knives,' he said.

It was a good story and one that improved when I asked Martha if we had done any stories previously about the meatworks. The lack of a filing system at the *Weekly Advertiser* was more than compensated for by Martha's elephantine memory –

and she also had a brother who worked on the mutton chain at the plant. Yes, she said slowly, she would talk to him for me.

The meatworks had been established in the last century on a site that had been far from town. Laxity of control had meant houses had spread outwards and around the plant in the intervening years, presenting a dilemma for town leaders. Unable to stop the residential spread following the rural buoyancy of the earlier decades, they had to endure complaints such as Pat's. The meatworks were a large and traditional employer, not to mention a necessary service industry for the region, and there was also the fact that Mr Nolan was a Shire councillor.

As manager of the meatworks, he lorded over the lives of his staff. As a Shire councillor he was a friend of old man Tilson, who referred to him as Mr Nolan. Mr Nolan was never known as anything but Mr Nolan – bar a few choice nicknames used by his workers among themselves. A man of iron resolve and little patience, he faced the world as a large, unshakeable mass. He would have cut up into some prime rump in his own plant if such things were allowed.

Under his rule the meatworks had rarely seen industrial troubles. But, times being what they were, and work being what it was, the bubble had burst. A phone-call from Martha's brother had proved that.

We agreed to meet outside the plant the next morning. He was waiting by the high wire fence a few minutes before the change of shifts. He handed me a pair of white overalls and a white paper hat. He was grim-faced and when he spoke it was softly and as a conspirator – 'I've an extra pair of wellingtons in my locker. I'll give them to you when we get inside. Look away from the guard on the gate as we walk past.'

Out on the killing floor it was every bit as bad as I had imagined. There had not been the time between shifts to hose down the walls of the room and it was awash with blood and debris. The big open channels designed to carry away the muck were clogged and spilling over on to the floor where the men worked. What had been designed to be a room hygienically cool had become heated with the mass of men and animals wrestling against time, death and decay.

The animals were herded in singly at one end of the room, released through a grille gate from the noisy holding pen behind. The noise and the scent of blood panicked them into a fear that either made them immobile or sent them into a series of frantic contortions as they tried to back out against the grille gate. A group of men held them steady while they were stunned with a bolt to the head, between the eyes. It sometimes took several efforts before they toppled with a crumple of legs, kicking wildly and dangerously and shitting copiously. Senseless, they were tackled up on to the overhead conveyor track and pushed towards the men who sliced deft slashes along the exposed, down-hanging throats.

Each time there came the sudden explosion of blood, a warm jet that released clouds of steam. The wild twitching and writhing of the dying nerves gave each carcass an eerie second life – a final protest – before the beast was swung along the track to drain some more. Further along, sharp knives would slice the stretched belly from anus to throat, and the spilling guts would cascade down into the collection vats.

There was a panic to it all. Animals electric with fear were slaughtered by men hard-pressed to cope with the flow. There was no pause to their work, no banter above the noise and no joy in the task at all.

I took a long shower, trying to scrub the thoughts from my mind.

'It's hard at first,' said Martha's brother, 'but it's money. Some blokes never learn to cope with the lambs or the vealers – they reckon it's like killing babies. Probably is.'

'Are they losing many stock out in the holding paddocks?'

'Thousands,' he said, towelling himself down. 'Dehydration more than anything. The watering system went bung yesterday – again. System can't cope with the demand. We'll go and have a look there, too.'

We scouted the outer edge of the holding paddocks on the way back to the gate. The ground was brown dirt, completely bare of grass. It had been beaten hard by the countless number of hoofs. Nor was there a tree around to shade the paddocks. From the shifting mass of animals I could see the weakest unable to lift their heads, which some were already on their sides and one or two had died with their legs sticking out stiffly. There was a thick, black swarm of flies in the air and around the eyes and tails of the stock.

'Fly strike would bother that lot,' I noted.

'Doesn't much matter,' said Martha's brother, pointing over the paddock to a truck fitted with block and tackle. A small group of men were winching aloft the bloated body of a cow. 'Dog food on four legs. That's about all.'

My first approach to Mr Nolan failed. The phone-call I made was answered by his secretary, a terse-sounding woman who would not let me speak to her boss.

'He's out,' she said, the ice gathering about her words.

'Do you know when he'll be back?'

'No.'

'Perhaps if I phoned back in an hour?'

'I don't know.'

'This afternoon perhaps?'

'I don't know.'

'Could I leave my name and phone number?'

'He's busy all day.'

'Could I leave them nevertheless?' She rang off too quickly to allow me to tell her.

I tried again within the hour, and within the next, and the next. Each time I was unable to breach the telephone fortress. Obstruction like this is all grist to the reporter's mill and I knew it well enough not to be annoyed. It was, in fact, a spark to the fire. I asked Pat to help me out.

'Hello, is Mr Nolan there?' Pat hung on the phone. 'Yes, you can tell him it's Mr Tilson calling... Thank you.' He winked at me, gave a thumbs-up and handed me the receiver.

'Hello, Mr Nolan?' I winked back at him. 'It's the *Weekly Ad.* here.'

Pat winced as I held the receiver away from my ear.

'I'm sorry about that,' I said. 'Your secretary must have switched me through by mistake. I'd been waiting on the phone for quite a while. I was phoning to get your thoughts about this industrial action up there at the meatworks. I believe a lot of farmers are being inconvenienced by it.'

Pat made a loud sucking noise. I waved him away.

'Yes, I see. If you don't wish to discuss it on the phone, perhaps I could come around and see you then? This afternoon? Fine, fine. Good. I'll see you then.' I slapped down the phone triumphantly. Pat slapped his thighs and did a quick jig around my office.

'Go get 'im.' he said.

*

The guard watched me with interest as I approached the gate. Mr Nolan was standing there ready for me when I arrived, and I realised he had no intention of letting me wander further into the plant than past the guard-house. The wire gates opened and shut for me. The place looked like a concentration camp. The meeting had the atmosphere of a showdown in an old Hollywood western.

His secretary stood at his side, her shorthand notebook poised to record the conversation and a sullen scowl cemented over her face. I smiled at her with all the charm I could summon.

'Good afternoon,' I said.

'Good afternoon,' he said, squinting hard at me against the light. 'What do you want to know?'

'Well, my understanding is that this whole issue has arisen from the increased demand on the works by farmers culling stock in the drought.'

'Yes.'

'What sort of increase have you had in your killing rate?'

'Quite a bit.'

'What . . . say, twenty per cent?'

'Something like that.'

'More? Thirty per cent?'

'Yes.'

'More than forty?'

'Probably not.'

'So between thirty and forty per cent increase in beef and mutton chains?'

'Bit less for mutton.'

'And have you taken on more staff to cope?'

'Few.'

'What, fifty men?'

'Bit less.'

'Thirty?'

'Look, I'm here to answer questions, not barter figures. I've got more important things to do. I don't have to talk to you.'

'I appreciate that fact. Have you asked the farmers to redirect stock?'

'It'd only mean more handling. Animals would lose condition.'

'But they're waiting around in the holding paddocks here already losing condition,' I said.

'You can't stop that. It happens whether there's a strike or not.'

'But I believe a larger number of animals than normal are affected.'

He snorted in annoyance, swatted at a fly and hitched up his trousers. 'Stock are dying all over the place, whether it's here or out on the farms. Farmers are asking us to slaughter for market and we're only trying to cope. This action by the men is harming the animals, sure, but they're only hurting themselves by going out. That's all I want to say. And they're fools if they think I'm going to budge.'

'Excuse me, Mr Nolan.' The guard at the gate was yelling at us. Behind the gate was a swarm of bodies all too recognisable for the video cameras plastered with television station stickers.

'Mr Nolan?' one of them called. 'Damian Watts here from Channel Nine News. Could we come in and have a word with you, please?'

'What the . . . ?' Nolan muttered beneath his breath.

'We heard about the action the men are taking and wondered how you're coping with the livestock stranded here,' the television reporter bellowed through the gate.

'Are you planning to ship the animals elsewhere?' came another voice from behind the fence.

'Are you aware that the RSPCA has been called in over the matter?' came another.

'Bugger off!' Mr Nolan bellowed back at them like an enraged bull.

'But Mr Nolan, we need your side of the dispute,' bleated one.

'How many stock have died in the past twenty-four hours, sir?'

'Bugger off, the lot of you,' Mr Nolan yelled back.

'But this is an important story if the RSPCA has been called in to investigate, sir.'

The reporter called Damian Watts yelled, 'Mr Nolan, we came up here by chartered plane. We've had to catch a taxi all the way from Nooweep.'

'Well then, you can catch it back,' Mr Nolan said. 'I'll only talk to the local press,' he added, clasping at my arm. 'And the rest of you can just piss off.'

'Have you got that?' Damian Watts was talking to his

cameraman. 'This is a boycott, a shut-out. Get a shot of him talking to the reporter of the local rag.'

I simply smiled at the camera, and Mr Nolan, I believe, did the same. Cameras of any sort always have that effect on people. As we smiled, Damian Watts lowered his trousers, turned around and showed us his white buttocks of protest. He was obviously miffed.

The others burst out laughing and we joined in. We were still laughing as they turned away, piled themselves and their gear into the taxi cabs and roared away in a flurry of dust and disgust.

The guard was shaking his head in disbelief. Mr Nolan took some time to stop laughing. He looked at me, smiling. 'And you can piss off too,' he growled, before turning heel and stalking back to the plant.

A Case for Dr Forbes

The players from both sides had given up many hours ago, with the first innings barely finished. The glare rising from the earth had made the batsmen scowl into the sun. The ground beneath had baked brick-hard so that the bowlers' feet hurt. They reduced their run-up to a short limp and then to a standing start. The shirts of the slipmen clung wet to their back, and the outfielders had now simply given in and strolled away. Scattered between the drinkers, the players had stripped down to white trousers. They were bare and brown-chested.

As close and stinking as it was beneath the heavy white canvas, it was all the more intolerable for those playing on the dry yellow turf and wincing under the heat of the day. The women out there, clustered in the shaggy shade of the few trees on the rim of the oval, fanned paper plates and newspapers at disgruntled children, trying to stir a draught from the lifeless air. And they flapped their soft, fleshy arms to cool their armpits so that, from this distance, they looked like a flock of overfed and grounded birds.

Around me, the gaps between the bodies were thickly filled with heat and noise. It was a brave man to shoulder into the mass of it and a fool to have stayed there.

Pat passed with a foaming jug held high over his head.

'Like the cattleyards on stock-market day,' I said.

'Yeh, just as much bull about,' he said, jabbing a sandwich in my mouth. 'Here, have a sandwich. Chicken. Battery hen, probably. Know the feeling?' And he was gone – swallowed up in the crowd.

Some hopeful had tried to get a barbecue going. A Rotarian, probably. The barbecue was a protracted and particularly cruel torture, a ritual of summer. Other races of the world require acts of strength to prove valour: running the gauntlet of ravines, polar ice-caps or maddened buffalo. In these parts the proof of manhood demanded the skills of building up a fire and using it to render otherwise acceptable slabs of meat into an unrecognisable and indigestible mass of char. Someone got one going – for a barbecue had been promised for the day. There could have been no other reason, and after a short period of labouring over the flames the effort was abandoned. The fire was left to gutter out while the defeated cook retired to the beer tent to replace some of the lost body moisture. As soon as the beer went in, it erupted through the pores. Good drinking weather it was, but not a day for big appetites.

It was a three-barrel afternoon that petered into a one-barrel night. The buffet of sandwiches and cakes prepared by the ladies of the cricket club auxiliary was eaten only in the cool of the evening.

One of my tasks of the following day was to document the offerings: three rounds of tomatoes, a box of lettuce and twenty-two roast chickens were consumed by the crowds that day. It was just about morning-tea time, just as I reached for my second coffee, when justice recalled its own.

It stirred up the deeper regions of my colon, whipped them into a multi-coloured mass and sent it heaving in both directions. I bolted for the toilet. It was locked. Thumping the door in frustration, I was answered with a muffled groan.

'Hurry up in there,' I yelled, and then clamped my teeth together.

The groan came again, dying at the edges like disappointment.

'Will you be long?'

It barely answered. The dying animal within had obviously reached the comatose state.

The muscles of my lower reaches were trying to grip against the tide, and I was swallowing hard. I gave the locked door a final belt and set off for the other toilet behind the print-room. The animal there was in loud and violent agony.

'Move it in there.' I believe I was starting to scream.

'I am.' The words drawled together before merging into a soft and spattering explosion.

I could wait no longer. I tapped gently at the door to the

women's toilet and stepped gingerly inside. To explain my predicament would have been altogether too embarrassing.

It came out both ends and left me panting and whitened. When my knees buckled I sank to the floor and sat there a good while, studying the unfamiliar surroundings and praying for inner peace. My thoughts were interrupted by hard knocking.

'For Chrissakes let us in.' The voice was male but strained into the higher reaches of falsetto. It was obviously in pain and under pressure.

It was enough to warrant a staff meeting. We all convened in the big print-room, a hang-dog bunch looking ashen-faced and haggard. There were some unsavoury smells around and more than one or two sudden disappearances.

'I'm sorry, but I can't let you all off sick today. We've a paper to put out,' said Hegarty, looking no less uncomfortable than the rest of us.

'But we're dying, boss.'

'Dying fast.'

'I reckon I'm dying slow. Very bloody slow.'

'I think I've brought up my appendix. What does an appendix look like?'

Someone started a lurid description that sent another three bodies hurtling for the toilets.

'Perhaps it was just a piece of tomato, then...'

'We've still got a paper to bring out,' Hegarty continued. 'We've published this paper every week since eighteen eighty-three. We've weathered greater storms than this. There was the war, and the other war, and the big drought of nineteen thirty-something...' He stopped to give a loud belch. He started to look greenish around the wattles. 'Excuse me,' he muttered. 'And our readers will be expecting a paper. They need their *Weekly Advertiser*...'

'... when they run out of toilet paper,' added some bright spark. 'Prepare for a big print-run this week.'

Hegarty was off in the direction of his office. Martha grabbed the reins of the meeting and held them with a solid and unwavering hand. She was the sort of woman Boadicea would have admired.

'Were there any others who didn't go to the cricket club

social – like me?' She spoke in a voice smug with righteousness. It was difficult not to loathe her.

'Is there anyone who didn't eat anything there?'

No hands showed.

'Or not a lot?'

It was still silent. The ranks of haggard faces presented a living, grimacing exercise in self-pity.

'You can't keep a sick man working. It's not fair,' ventured one voice.

'But a hung-over man deserves what he gets,' she lashed back, with the stuff to make an Amazon flinch.

'Shit a brick.' The mutter of disbelief came low and from the direction of Pat.

'I already have.' The reply came from Hegarty as he re-entered the room. 'With nails in it. But I'm staying here to work and so are you all.' He turned on an unsteady heel and staggered back to his office, shutting the door behind him and doubtless collapsing into his chair for a recuperative sleep.

The hospital confirmed it. They had received calls from anguished citizens all morning, and Matron was fast running low on antacids and patience.

'No, Dr Forbes is not in,' she replied tetchily. 'And no – I do not know when he'll be back.'

'Could I leave a message please?' From the sound of my drawn voice it could well have been my last words.

'I'm a very busy woman at the moment, sir.'

'And I'm making this call under great duress, Matron.'

'More strength to your sphincter. I'll tell him you called. Drink plenty of fluids.'

'Thank you, Matron,' I said, reaching for a fourth cup of tea brought by Martha, who had transformed from an Angel of Doom to a Guardian Angel, ferrying countless cups to dehydrated workers and making repeated aspirin runs to the medicine cabinet. The sort of woman who would have done well in the trenches, that one. She earned for herself a sort of backhand admiration.

Few men made it to Molloy's for lunch, and those who did spent their time wisely, discussing remedies ranging variously from Royal Jelly to an indecent concoction involving a raw egg. One sufferer was coaxed into a glass of crème de menthe and lemonade – a cocktail that settled his stomach like a stiff easterly chop to the Bay of Biscay. He didn't surface from the toilets for the rest of the afternoon, but was found to be breathing. The rest of us merely settled for a glass or two of retribution.

'It could've killed us, that bloody chicken,' said one.

'You reckon that's what did it?'

'Bloody chicken sandwiches in that heat. Reckon so.'

'Do you think this is what it feels like to be a ghost?'

'Nah... ghosts wouldn't feel as bad as this.'

'I figure I'd sink through a few walls if you pushed me. I feel that weak.'

'Anyway... ghosts are dead.'

'So?'

Dr Forbes was in surgery that afternoon and had patients to visit in the evening, so Matron said. A few of the older people had come down really badly and were causing the good doctor more than the usual amount of concern. She didn't know what time he'd be finishing but predicted it would be late. Being the sole medico in a stricken town would be a task of frightening responsibility. Like that three-week spate of births nine months after the church social when the vicar made a mistake with the port and the fruit punch.

The phone in the doctor's surgery continued to ring unanswered. By the following day there was news already that several elderlies had been taken to the base hospital at Nooweep overnight. One or two of their number were said to be in a serious state – Pat's grandfather being in that number. He was looking slightly distraught when I caught up with him outside his camera-room.

'Yeh, doesn't look too good for the poor old blighter,' he said, kicking at a loose piece of floor tile. 'They had the drip in him already when they loaded him into the meat van.'

'Will he be all right?'

'Can't really tell.'

'Was he conscious?'

'He was talking.'

'What did he say?'

'He touched my hand gently as the ambulance guys strapped him on to the stretcher, and told me, "Number five in the third race on Saturday."' He shook his head slowly and scuffed at the floor. 'Not a hope. Poor old guy. That horse fell at its last two races. The old bastard's losing his touch and I when

I heard him say that – then I knew he must be pretty bad.' He sucked air between his teeth, lifted his head and gave me a slow wink. 'So I did like he said. Never liked him much anyway.'

My hunt for Dr Forbes was not successful. He was clearly running a constant errand of mercy and I was obviously running foul of Matron's tolerance.

With my deadline hanging close, I decided to visit his house as the only way left to pin down the local medical authority for a few words.

One of the older and grander stone houses on the outskirts of town was home and surgery to Dr Forbes. He was a man of grey beard and grizzled appearance, squat, abrasive and sometimes rough of manner – but never of speech. His ancestors had come to Australia with others of Scottish ilk and, like them, had made considerable profit from the move. He employed a gardener and a housekeeper to help his wife. He employed a young girl to stand behind his surgery counter in a fetching uniform.

'Oh yes, he's in,' she said.

'That's fortunate. I've been having trouble phoning him.'

'Yes. He told me to take the phone off the hook.'

'Off the hook?'

'Oh yes,' she said with disarming charm. 'He's been... indisposed for most of the day. It's been very difficult.' She broke off and gazed at the toilet door.

'Is he in there now?'

She nodded. 'And most of the night, when he hasn't been visiting patients.'

'He's been doing a lot of visiting?'

'Quite a bit. He comes back here a lot to ... to ... But then he's out again. He really hasn't stopped.'

'It must be a great worry to him.'

'And Mrs Forbes.'

There was a flush. The door opened as a very weak Dr Forbes tottered out, leaned against the doorpost and then slowly straightened. The look about him was that of a man emerging from five stiff rounds of bare-knuckled boxing, or five stiffer nights on 100 per cent proof liquor. There was no colour in his skin save grey, and it seemed his face had been left unironed at the bottom of a wicker basket. It took almost all his energy to straighten up and glare at me.

'And so, what are you doing here?' It was less of a question than an accusation.

'I'm here for the story, Dr Forbes.'

'There is no story.'

'I believe there is.'

'On what grounds?' He was really putting up a fight.

'On the strength that so many people in the town have been ill.'

'I can't discuss it. Medical histories are confidential.'

'But this relates to a public function. And that isn't.'

He pursed his lips and dropped his head a moment. He looked at the girl. 'I'll take a cup of tea in my room, and one for the gentleman too,' he said. I followed him in and caught the tail-end of a low-pitched fart he made and ignored. He opened a window and lowered himself delicately into a chair. I did likewise, for fear that the muscle cramps would double me over again.

'Could you tell me how many people you estimate are affected?' I began.

'Affected by what?' he said, opening a bottle of tablets and emptying a few into his palm.

'By this stomach upset.'

'Would you like some? They're quite harmless but they seem to make me feel better.' He offered some tablets.

'No, thank you. I'm all right if I don't move too quickly.' And in saying so, and in merely thinking about my bowels, I added, 'May I use your ... ?'

He nodded and waved to the door, swallowing the tablets with a dry gulp.

I returned to find tea waiting and the remnants of yet more flatulence hanging pungently in the air.

'Perhaps you could warn people about the hazards of food preparation in hot weather,' I suggested, sitting slowly.

'Why would I do that?'

'As a response to this bout of food poisoning.'

'How do you know it's food poisoning? There's nothing to prove that it's food poisoning.' His brows crossed and met in the centre of his forehead. 'Nothing at all.' He spoke with a surprising determination. I realised that his eyebrows were actually touching. 'It could be one of many things. A virus, some pathogenic infection spread by close contact. There are a great number of gastric irritations spread by all kinds of ubiquitous organisms...' His native burr was becoming more pronounced. 'Nothing has been proven. You can quote that.'

'But coincidence would suggest...'

'... that pathological investigation is needed. One does not jump to conclusions in medical science. When one is dealing with such cases one must undertake a variety of tests to eliminate all possibilities. You can quote that too,' he said, stopping to burp.

'I can understand that,' I said. I was encountering more difficulties than I had foreseen. The old man was getting quite churned up over it all. He was also farting more copiously.

'You will have to excuse me.' He was out of the room a long time and when he came back he looked most uncomfortable.

'So you can't confirm that it was food poisoning?'

'I can't.'

'Pardon me, but I find that difficult to understand. Everyone who attended that cricket club party, and of those everyone who ate the chicken sandwiches...' I belched.

'And I may I suggest to you, sir, that you are jumping to conclusions.' He did not chance sitting down again and hovered angrily over me. 'I'm a very busy man. And there was a great deal of alcoholic beverage drunk at that event. There are well-documented cases of what a surfeit of liquor can do to the alimentary canal' – he looked at me closely – 'and to the brain cells' – he looked at me yet more closely – 'with which, doubtless, members of your profession are well acquainted.'

'It surely can't be a mass hangover.'

'It can't be anything at the moment, but there are also cases of psychosomatic illnesses on a large scale. Hysterias.'

'Are you saying it could be auto-suggestion?'

'More or less. People have been known to assume symptoms.'

I stared hard at him. It was difficult to take it all in and just as difficult keeping it all in.

'And perhaps one or two of those claiming to be affected are merely suffering one of the most common complaints of the modern day – sloth, sir. A prolonged and opportunistic bout of lassitude.' He was becoming more pointed, and more flatulent.

'You mean they could be faking it? All those people?'

He spread his hands. 'Or a virus.'

'When will you know for sure?'

'When the results come back from the laboratory at Nooweep Hospital.'

'When will that be?'

'When I send them.'

'You mean you haven't sent them yet?'

'I've told you, I'm a very busy man.'

'But won't the samples have degraded and the bugs broken up in this time?' Disbelief was now pummelling at my powers of reasoning.

'I've told you, I'm a busy man,' he said. 'It's late and I have patients to attend.' The burr of his voice was now a buzz of annoyance. He motioned me to the door and vanished quickly elsewhere before I reached it.

The sound of the door brought the young girl out of her office.

'You off then?'

'Yes. Dr Forbes is a little – engaged – at the moment.'

The girl giggled softly, smoothing her face over with her hand.

'Poor man,' I offered.

'And his poor wife,' she said. 'She's so ashamed about it. She's not shown her head out of this house ever since. Poor woman. I had to do her shopping yesterday – she was too embarrassed to go into town. Poor woman. She'll never live it down.'

'Yes,' I said, shielding the uncertainty in my voice lest it reveal my ignorance. I sensed an answer pending with just a little prompting and a touch of spice. 'But it's only the first time that it's happened.'

'Oh yes.' The enchanting creature took the bait delightfully. 'And she's been working at the club catering for so many years. It was just bad luck I suppose.'

'Yes. Bad luck.'

'I mean, if they'd asked her to do the teas, or the cakes, or even the other sandwiches, none of this would have happened. Or not to her.'

'But chicken...'

'Yes, chicken. You can never be sure with chicken.' We shook our heads – me with my newly profound knowledge of dietary hygiene and the doctor's wife. There was a solid flush of water.

'I'd better be on my way. He's a very busy man, you know,' I said.

'Yes. A poor man, really,' said the girl.

Sin City

Some men with lives of fame and danger hanker for suburban domesticity. They grow foxgloves, or collect stamps, or make ocean liners out of matchsticks, all in the fractured logic of keeping sane. And those people living a life more predictable and parochial sometimes turn foolhardy with the hunger for excitement.

The steering wheel was vibrating in Tam's hands as he pushed the accelerator further down to the floor. The gathering speed of the car sent up a whine of wind that rose to a shriek. I could see every bone in my hand standing out from the tightness of my fist as it clenched hard to the dashboard. The road was straight and empty and the car lurched from verge to gravel verge in wide, loopy swerves. Tam sent up war-whoops of delight.

After a while my nerves unwound and I joined in with his laughter. I was going back for a break in Melbourne and I didn't care. A weekend away meant a weekend of freedom to perform all the gross indecencies. I intended to return from Melbourne a very old man – or at least feeling like one.

The roadside flashed past and merged into a single, blurred line of speed and colour. And still the car did not seem to be travelling half fast enough. The last flat stretch of volcanic plain seemed endless. In the distance, the city skyline thickened the horizon, then vanished with the shift in the road and re-emerged – beckoning all the while like a seasoned flirt. The buildings rose higher, the flat openness of the fields became dissected into neat and natty housing blocks and then into tight and hard-pressed factories. The sky all wide and clear in the country now became a fine grey, a beautiful colour to my eyes. It seemed stronger, more worldly-wise.

Tam gunned the car and ran a sequence of red lights. We both laughed: it was good to be back and we could hardly wait to hit the city centre. We cruised down through the corridors of the main streets. There was more colour here than I last remembered, and more variety in the faces. The buildings were taller and the trams noisier than I had remembered. All the brakes on all the buses needed a good oiling.

The wind channelled up from the docks was a fragrant mixture of diesel and salt. It swept past the dark brick warehouses on each bank and chipped at the water as it went. Catching stray newspapers, it heaved them apart and scattered them, so that they swirled and bowled along, moving as if suddenly possessed by a spirit.

We walked along the wharfs watching the gulls hanging over the water, dropping down as the air stream pulled apart before quickly soaring up on the next gust. Suspended over the water, they watched us with dispassionate eyes. Silky oil patches flung about on the restless river shone up pink, blue and green and the water itself reflected the grey sky.

There was the rattle of movement and the clatter of industry, metal screeched on metal and a goods train wormed past on silver rails. Deep down from the docks came the throaty hoot of a ship. And there was a whistle, loud and liquid, coming from the train tracks. Leaning over the edge of the railway bridge I saw a ganger sitting by the side of the tracks waiting and doing nothing in particular but whistling. The bright yellow flag he carried – the only slash of colour amid the grimy grey – he sometimes waved in time to his tune. He whistled and warbled a long time, taking a childish delight in it all.

'That's it. That's what I need,' said Tam, snapping his fingers. 'A canary!'

'But you've already got the budgie. And Samovar.'

'No, I need a canary. The miners had them for safety. I need an educated, urbane and witty canary well adjusted to all this modern life.'

'What's that?' I was starting to lose his meaning.

'Don't you see? Canaries are an early-warning system. The moment my canary tries to do itself in, the moment it starts to crack under the strain . . .'

I decided Tam had spent too long driving.

We strolled in between the buildings. It hardly seemed like a woman lying there in the sun with her possessions spilling out of the plastic bags gathered around her. She was lying curled up in a doorway close to the dock and the railway and she was sleeping oblivious to all the noise. The overstuffed bags were pillows for her gaunt limbs against the concrete. She had gathered them close to her for fear of pilferers. She cradled a car hub-cap and a couple of empty plastic bottles.

We walked past her and looked back. She had been watching us and had one eye open. The other was filmy, the eyelids were fat and red, inflamed with pus. I felt a dry retch rise in me and we quickly walked on.

I drove the car through the suburbs. Tam spent most of the trip with his nose flattened to his window. 'Salmon pink, salmon pink,' he chanted. 'Why do they paint nearly every house salmon pink?'

'It must be this year's fashionable colour,' I said.

'Salmon pink, salmon spawn, salmon vomit, salmon phlegm – horrible, just horrible,' he said, pulling the jumper over his head. 'Tell me when we're there.'

Friday evening descended on the city after a day made longer by the heat. Commuters swarmed the pavements in the headlong dash for the next train to carry them out of the steaming city and into air-conditioned suburbia. They packed thickly along the paths, sometimes spilling out on to the roads where they dodged between cars and trucks snarled in traffic jams. Young men covered the last stretch to the station in long, leggy sprints. Office girls, the vestal handmaidens to Commerce, tottered past on high-heeled shoes, quick-stepping over the uneven pavement. The crowd surged wherever the tide broke before them, like the first race of salmon in the mad, mindless flight to freedom. They flowed like liquid through the vast arch of Flinders Street Station.

The sun was sitting low in the sky, and its rays cast an intense golden light that cut through the hot haze of smoke and fumes to glint off the glass and chrome of the tightly packed traffic. Thick fingers of reddened cloud veiled the fire-ball red of the sun. The thought of a beer had never seemed more inviting, nor more apt. As I drove, I imagined the bright orange glare that such a sun would strike through a full glass. I was imagining holding the glass against the light and marvelling at the colours. Then I imagined drinking it. The first glass wouldn't even touch my sides, I told myself.

Watering hole of the workers, the Bricklayer's Arms had always stood high on a hill over the rail cutting and overlooking the river. The long, steep walk to its door had never yet deterred a man who would otherwise have called himself world-weary. Unpretentious and utilitarian, it had remained the same serviceable brown brick for as long as memory existed. As a small child I would watch the passage of the sun by the light that came through the frosted glass window and patterned the table with stipple. Dipping my finger into my lemonade I would mark the hourly advance of the light across the table while my father made careful effort to ignore it. The toilets, as I remembered, always smelled of fish, and a highlight of childhood memory was the day they cleaned the mildew off the walls. Long wooden benches ranged along the sides of the room. In my mind I could not visualise the place without a haze of drifting blue cigarette smoke suspended across the ceiling. The walls and floors were covered in linoleum tiles with grilles set in them so that the cleaners merely had to hose down the room for the next day's trading.

It opened at seven to comfort the workers of the dawn shifts and was there again at four in the afternoon to welcome them back. By eight it would be crammed to noisy, restless capacity with barely room for the pool players to bend over the table. Hopers drunk there, and no-hopers too; loners and extroverts; union bosses; Greeks; resident wits; long-distance lorry drivers; pawnbrokers; jockeys; meat merchants who boasted of the length and alacrity of their tools; greyhound trainers; gangers and railway shunters; veteran soldiers with aches in their joints and troubles in their waterworks; tram conductors; cleaners; punters hungry for a winning tip; ex-boxers; hangers-on; shysters and bookmakers who never spoke in loud voices, and conmen who did. There was, no doubt, much bullshit spun within its walls – it was the very mortar between the bricks and held the place together.

If a policeman were to turn up there it would only be for a short while. Even the police had the wisdom to leave well enough alone. Once or twice a plain-clothed detective might wander in, recognised immediately from his bearing and his haircut. They would be tolerated but not welcomed, and most got the hint after the first drink.

It was a clean shop, run by publican Frank, known as 'Piles' because he was 'a pain in the bum'. His taps were clean, his beer was good and Piles had a knack of employing barmaids born to the task.

'So, you say this is a good pub,' said Tam, leaning into the slope on the rise to the door. 'This bloke Piles sounds pretty good. Bricklayer's Arms – honest name.'

I could not answer, but stood frozen to the spot, blinking and staring like a myopic owl. Spotlights angled over the striped canvas awning stretched out over the front door. Above it, a panel of flashing lights played lurid colours and spelled out 'Thick as the Brick' in garish fluorescence. The frosted windows had been replaced by wide expanses of glass showing the milling crowd within. The heaving sea of bodies was lit by the swirl of multi-coloured disco lights. From the open doors came a ground-shaking thump of rock music and the high-pitched babble of people yelling at each other. And the building had been repainted . . . salmon pink.

'Oh hell, Tam. I'm sorry. It's changed. For the worse.'

'I can see that even without subtitles,' he said.

'I can't believe it. Why would Piles do it?'

'Money perhaps? Happens that way.'

We stood and watched the crowd within. There were young women almost wearing dresses and writhing to the pulse of the music. Men with chest hair and gold pendants stamped and bobbed their heads in rhythm. It all looked like some absurd mating ritual between members of a primitive tribe waiting for the tourists to throw coins.

'Well?' I said. 'Do you still want a drink?'

'After climbing that hill, yes,' said Tam. 'But . . .' His voice trailed off as he watched the mob.

'You could always drink it like medicine, with your eyes shut,' I said.

'Fair enough.'

Walking through the wall of sound, I felt a stranger on home ground. The close and cosy space of the main bar had been pulled open into a large, single room blaring movement and colour. The dowdy glory of the wooden bar had been torn away and now glared angry black and orange plastic under bright lights. Bottles of sherry and port that had spent years on distant shelves gathering dust had gone. A wall of mirrors reflected ranks and ranks of up-ended bottles holding a rainbow of coloured liquors. It was a cornucopia of hangovers and as welcoming as a minefield. Anyone drinking a blue cocktail deserves sinuses of unset concrete the next morning.

The hardy old lino tiles had gone, replaced by a thick patterned carpet that sank soggily under-foot as we breasted the bar. Gone too were the barmaids of legend and outstanding natural assets. Where Nina had once held court, dispensing lager and personal advice, stood slim and dapper young men looking flustered and uncomfortable in bow ties. They rushed from dispenser to dispenser, tossing together brightly coloured measures of frightening potency and topping the glasses with prissy swizzle sticks and paper umbrellas. These they served most to young women, who giggled as their escorts handed over the money in exchange.

The music merged into a single throb that made it impossible to distinguish between one record and the next. From time to time a loud male voice full of breathy growls and decibels thundered across the room before the music restarted. The writhing bodies were packed in close and there seemed to be a lot of screaming.

Tam stood at the bar dispassionately picking his nose and waiting for service. It came in a rush.

'Two beers. Hold the maraschino cherries, thanks,' said Tam.

We edged back from the bar, afraid the gyrating dancers would knock our drinks. Tam looked around slowly with disdain warping his face, and then, seeing two empty seats, made a lizard-flick of a jump for them.

He motioned me to lean towards him and, cupping his hand around my ear bellowed, 'Bosch.'

'Wassat?' I yelled back.

'Hieronymus Bosch ... coming down from a bad night's tripping,' he said, waving his arms airily around. 'With a place like this, who needs Armageddon?'

'Armagh who?'

'Geddon ... Armageddon.' He was starting to stare angrily at me. I decided to just nod energetically.

'It's really much of a muchness,' he bellowed. 'Evolution in fast rewind. Isn't science wonderful?'

An expensive-looking woman sitting near by leaned over and yelled at me, 'I think your friend's fighting a losing battle.'

I nodded.

Tam leaned across the table and screamed, 'What did she say?'

I waved him off, shaking my head. He tapped the woman's hand, gesturing her to lean across the table so that he could yell in her ear.

'Puberty? What do you mean by puberty?' she shrieked back.

He shook his head for a moment, pushed closer to her ear and yelled his words slowly and singly. She laughed, fluttering her fingers in front of her face and falling back into her chair.

The man sitting beside her had been watching the dancers, and turned to her. Amid her giggles, she tried to scream in his ear, pointing at Tam. The man leaned across the table to him, cupping his hands and bellowing.

'Yes,' Tam screamed back. 'Bosch.' And away it all went again. I could only sit back and watch the futile assault of conversation against the cacophony. I picked out 'moral decadence' and 'Edward Gibbons'. They were doing a lot of nodding and bobbing, but seemed to be enjoying themselves.

'Do you want a drink?' I thundered at the woman.

She nodded, pushing forward her and her companion's glasses. 'Dry white with spritz.'

'With what?' I yelled.

'Spritz.'

I shook my head. Her companion took over. 'Spritz,' he said, with a vigour that irrigated my ear. 'They put a squirt of soda in it. Very cooling. You mustn't be a regular here.'

Light reflected from the bar caught his face, and I squinted hard at it for it bore a familiarity. The drooping moustache and the gleaming pearly-whites could have adorned any car salesman or Test cricketer, but I fitted the piece to the puzzle, grabbed the glasses and escaped to the bar to consider my reaction.

We put back a lot of drink that night. Our throats, roughened from yelling, demanded regular lubrication, and for his round the man returned from the bar with large glasses of advocaat mixed with something vaguely toxic. It went down very smoothly, as did the next.

'Better than a glass of congealed pork fat,' yelled Tam, taking the glasses to the bar. 'Mind my seat.'

'What did he say?' yelled the woman.

When they were handing out perversity of spirit, Tam must have gone back for second helpings. He arrived at the table with large glasses of something dangerously close to cherry brandy. 'Get this in you,' he thundered. 'The Queen drinks this, and look what it's done for her.' He grabbed a glass, took a breath and up-ended it with a gulp. He waited for us to follow suit. That reminded us of tequila, and soon a jug of clear poison and a plate of sliced lemon arrived at our table.

'You probably won't remember this.' I had my arm wound around the man's shoulders. It had got suddenly heavy and I found it easier to lean my weight against him. 'But I've met you before.'

'Wassat?' He was leaning his weight back on me and the pair of us sat there in an uneasy and unstable sort of equilibrium.

'You're Damian Watts – the terrorvision guy, right?'

'The what guy?'

'The . . .' I shut my eyes and concentrated. ' . . . terrorvision guy. Reporter – right?'

He nodded slowly, giving a lop-sided smile.

'I saw you once. Behind a wire fence.'

'What doing?'

'Pardon? What did you say?' I yelled.

'What doing?' He burped and held still for a moment. His head was swaying backwards and forwards.

'You were . . . ah, nothing. Nothing much. Just saw you, that's all.'

'What?' he cupped his ear closer.

'Nothing, nothing . . . I just saw you . . . on terrorvision.'

'Terrorvision!' He snorted a laugh that percolated his drink on to his moustache. 'You hear that?' He elbowed Tam. 'He called it terrorvision.'

'Is there any other kind?' said Tam.

'Was he say?' bawled the woman, her stockinged feet lifted up on to the table. 'Who's the next shout?' she bellowed in a voice raw and sharp enough to coleslaw granite at fifty paces. 'Who'll buy a drink for a lady?'

*

The Sèvres collection in the glass-fronted cabinet wasn't mine. Nor the elephantine vase bursting over with roses. Turning my head, I heard the rustle of the ruched satin cushion under my head. Daylight welled in through the large paned windows, danced off the highly polished table and was lost in the vastness of the room. There was a cavernous fireplace edged with a marble mantelpiece which carried a couple of figurines reflected in a mirror. Magazines piled over a side table had photographs of elegant women and gun dogs.

The walls, of soft green, picked out the colours of the chairs flanking the fireplace. They were large, box-like and obscenely overstuffed, and I had a faint memory of spilling my drink over one of the arms.

There was a black plastic bucket beside the couch, near my head, with a fat white towel folded near by and a tray with a carafe of water and a glass. Next to them was a pile of neatly folded clothes. They were the clothes I had been wearing yesterday. Was it yesterday? I could not remember removing them and folding them so neatly. My underpants were draped gently on the top of the pile.

I reached under the rug tossed over me. Yes, they were my underpants.

Somewhere, from behind several closed doors, I could hear movement and the faintest sound of an operatic aria joined intermittently by a female's humming. It drew nearer, stopping with the soft click of the door leading into the room. The face that appeared was powder soft and framed by wisps of hair. It was more a suggestion of a face, washed clean of colour, translucent and unmarked as Lalique.

'Good morning,' the mouth said.

'Good morning.' I sounded as though I had spent the night sandpapering my vocal chords.

'I'll arrange breakfast,' she said, and disappeared.

I sat staring at the door for a long time, shook myself awake and pulled on some clothes.

A tray rattling softly with dishes came into the room and she placed it on the table. I went to reach for my shirt, uncertain if it was belated modesty or not.

A cluster of china dishes patterned with flowers nestled alongside a collection of silverware. She took cups and poured coffee in them. Handing me one, she folded into the chair beside me, waiting for me to talk. I couldn't even remember her name.

There was gold looped several times around her neck and burying into the folds of her blouse. She was fine-boned and long-limbed. There was a plain gold ring on her finger and her nails were curiously blunt, cut square at the edges.

'You slept well?' she asked.

'Yes.' I watched the face, seeking in its clarity some suggestion of where I was, how I had come to be here and what I had done. 'It is . . . Sunday, isn't it?'

'Yes. You really weren't very well last night, were you?'

I stared at the eggs, the toast rack, the butter curls. 'I'm afraid I may have . . .'

She relaxed into a smile. 'You did nothing untoward.'

My relief came in a rush of breath. 'Oh, then I didn't . . .'

'I said you did nothing untoward.'

'Then I did?' An awful terror twanged in me.

'And it was not untoward.'

My mind couldn't keep pace. I stuffed a piece of toast in my mouth.

'And you probably don't even remember my name,' she said.

I tried to smile.

'Don't worry,' she said. 'It's probably best that way. My husband has already left for work. He had an early shift. That's why he went to bed early, remember?'

I could only nod and drain my cup of coffee. 'It's time for me to think about going, too,' I said.

'I would like you to stay, but I understand,' she said.

'Er . . . could you please tell me where I am?'

'It's all right. I'll call you a taxi while you dress.' She rose, smoothed her skirt and left the room smooth as cream.

The garden beyond the patio was long and green, shaded by thickets of birch and rhododendron. I was unsure if the tennis court was part of the property.

Her voice reappeared from the hall. 'You wanted to play tennis last night, some time around two a.m.'

'Tennis? I can't play tennis.'

'And then you took to howling at the moon. It was a full moon last night.'

'Howling?'

'You set off the guard dog and its barking woke the neighbours. They switched on their floodlights thinking there was a burglar about. You yelled things at them. The police paid a short visit. It seemed someone had phoned them.'

'And . . . your husband?'

'Slept through it. Slept through it all. My husband is a very heavy sleeper. He never hears anything – at all.'

A car horn sounded. 'Your cab is here, I shall show you out.'

Her skirt lay flat over her behind as she passed in front of me in the hall. Her calves were pleasantly fleshed and tapered smoothly. I believe I may even have smiled to myself.

On either side of the hall, portraits of ancestors long dead watched me pass. It was like running the gauntlet. I could feel their Victorian disapproval all along the long march to the heavy wooden front door.

She opened it, stood away and shook my hand. Over her shoulder was a studio portrait, she seated and her husband's hand on her shoulder. It was the television reporter. I stepped out. 'Thank you,' she said. 'I enjoyed your visit.'

Fanning Flames

Festive was not the word for it, but it was an occasion. The first polling day for the Nooweep Shire elections in more than twenty years was heralded with all the excitement this town could muster. The sun itself seemed to leap over the horizon, too full of anticipation to linger around the pinkness of the dawn.

It must have been a startling sight for those who sampled old man Tilson's generosity in Molloy's the previous night. He had commandeered the taps, ordering Mick to keep the glasses filled and tab ready – promising to settle the account at closing time. Heartened by this, the drinkers toasted the health of old man Tilson many times that evening. It was rough politics but effective. The odds that Pat was offering widened with each glass. For a two-horse race, the bets were heavily weighted against the challenger, and, to keep the punters' interest up, Pat had opened another book. So conclusive was the outcome of the election that Pat was taking bets not on the chances of a Tilson win, but on the size of it.

Tied to the fence around the school was a banner saying 'Polling Booth', and all around it that morning was a swarm of adults and children attracted by the novelty of the proceedings. The voters took their time with the democratic process, and stood around for a long time afterwards talking. The CWA made use of it, with its members manning a cake stall, and doing good business. The Fire Brigade had volunteers out with collection tins, as did the Red Cross and the football club. The Rotarians had a pie cart, the women of the church committee were running a raffle, and there seemed to be general agreement that elections were not such a bad thing after all.

Old man Tilson sailed through the crowd like a two-masted schooner in a fair wind. There was a clean-scrubbed redness to his face, and even the bald stretch of his forehead seemed to gleam as brightly in the sun as the war medals pinned to his chest. He laughed a lot, shaking hands and patting shoulders, and addressed everyone by their first names. He bought the biggest and most elaborate cream sponge from the CWA stall, making a good deal of noise as he did. He bought a wad of raffle tickets with a flourish of bank-notes, telling Mrs Warrington he expected first prize from so many tickets. Calling all the children together, he ordered soft drinks for them all, handing each one out with a laugh and a pat on the head. He laughed like a man taking unbridled pleasure in it all, doubtless confident of his right to do so.

Not once did he even cast a glance towards Nigs and Dianne, standing each side of the school gate with their pamphlets proffered limply to arriving voters. Nor did they look towards him, but stood there trying to pass the leaflets into others' hands and looking resigned at the repeated refusals.

Vivian tried to join the queue of children receiving drinks and stood around glumly kicking at the earth after his mother called him back.

'No, it's not Father Christmas. There is no Father Christmas,' she told him.

The crowds did not diminish during the day but swelled all the more as the clock neared five p.m. – the official closing time of the poll. It was a moment of high theatre when the Shire staff shut the doors to allow only scrutineers from both sides entry into the school. Nigs and Dianne walked in slowly, Vivian trailing behind, turning from time to time to look pointedly at the soft-drink van.

Silence drifted over the crowds outside as they settled down for the wait. Apart from hushed conversations rippling through the assembly, there seemed to be no restlessness. Even as they played, the children kept their voices muted. It was a moment of history, they had been told, and something they would remember for as many years as they drew breath. They observed the moment with childish solemnity.

When the doors re-opened, the hushed people filtered into the assembly hall of the school to hear the declaration of the polls. They drifted in through the doors and hung close to the walls, standing in silence. They left a respectable space between themselves and Nigs and Dianne. Vivian looked nonplussed and chewed at a tassel hanging from his mother's long flowered shawl. Her hand clutched at Nigs and her knuckles were white. They shared the same nervous set to their faces.

Peter Maddocks, the electoral returning officer and Shire Secretary, cleared a path through the crowd and undertook a lengthy and noisy performance of clearing his throat. Small and weedy, looking not the least bit phlegmatic, his efforts were obviously more theatrical than therapeutic. It only took a few seconds.

'... duly appointed returning officer for the west riding of Nooweep Shire...' His voice stayed flat as he read the totals – Tilson had won, although Dianne's defeat had been far from absolute. The cheers went up in patches and the assembly turned to each other with a certain surprise, each voter wondering who had been the turncoats as they pattered out their applause for the victor.

Old man Tilson gave a slight smile, wrapped one arm around Mrs Tilson and with the other gave a wave to acknowledge the applause. Even he looked a mite surprised. He also looked ruddy, and there was every indication that he had accepted a few fortifiers earlier in the afternoon. In fact, he weaved visibly as he approached Dianne with an outstretched hand to offer his most profound, and public, condolences.

As he walked up to the woman he thought how bedraggled she looked. His palm reached out for hers. And that restaurant bloke beside her could have done with a shave and a haircut. Then a wave of red struck his eyeballs and raced back into his brain. There was a high squeal in his ears and a pain like an iron bar thumped against his chest. The room of people saw him stagger backwards, reel around and collapse to the floor.

Old man Tilson writhed in wordless discomfort as the nurse holding the catheter gently inched it in. The nurse holding his left arm had a grip far stronger than the one holding his right. He could not reach the damnable itch under his left nostril where the plastic drainage tube rubbed at his skin. The roseola heat rash that had blossomed under his armpits stung with his sweat, and he smelled like nothing on earth. He ground his teeth as the tube went in deeper, flexed and unflexed his toes and stared like an angry man at the slow-turning fan on the ceiling above him.

He was tired of pain. He was tired of being tired. He had been sleeping badly and dreaming things of great evilness. Churches mainly, empty stone churches with Gothic arches, and silent save for the sound of the machine beside his bed. He had kept an ear constantly alert for that sound. Sliding in and out of sleep, he had struggled to catch the next high-pitched bleep as proof that his stricken heart had not stopped for all time. He heard the intervals between the signals, intervals where time was elastic and silence was ominous.

He needed a shave, he wanted to fart. The thick scent of the flowers by his pillow sickened and frightened him. He could have gone a cold beer.

He winced. 'Mr Tilson, I've told you already. You must stay very, very still,' the nurse rebuked him.

The overhead fan kept rhythm with the monitor beside him, and he counted slowly with each revolution: one-click-bleep-two-click-click . . .

It must have been within the same ten minutes as the ward sister noticed the alarm light that Dianne Westgrove took the Bible in her right hand.

'Please repeat after me . . .' Peter Maddocks was beginning the induction of the new councillor.

News had spread quickly of fate's quirky ways: of old man Tilson's coronary and the election by default of the woman from the city. In its wake came many faces, and many unknown faces, into the RSL hall that afternoon. It was crowded. Extra chairs were ranged along the walls and packed tightly to the doors. Spilling out of the doors and on to the steps, the people outside craned and weaved for a better view. I could see Vivian high astride the shoulders of Nigs, and beyond them Tam was idling against a parked car. He seemed to be testing the door lock.

There had never been such interest, nor so many bodies present, at a Council meeting, and the eleven wise men elected by their peers now looked uncomfortably accountable. Pushed tightly into suits and ties brushed off and newly donned for the occasion, they looked as grim as a row of Easter Island statues.

They shifted in their seats and kept their attention on Dianne as she carefully repeated the oath.

'... and allegiance to God and the Queen ...'

Dianne did not repeat the words of the Shire Secretary.

'... and allegiance to God and the Queen,' he repeated pointedly.

'I'm sorry, but I can't swear to that on oath,' she said.

'I beg your pardon.'

'I have no faith in any God and feel I bear no allegiance to a British monarch.'

The vast chasm of silence slowly filled with noise. At first it was a murmur, then it swelled up into a din, then it burst over into yells. It pushed and shoved at the mass of bodies, driving them forwards towards the Council bench. Councillors leapt away from their chairs, and those too slow found themselves toppling under the surging wave of protest. One, as he fell, grabbed wildly at the curtain and collapsed beneath the folds of fabric that tore away in his hand. As it fell, it caught the Union Jack, bringing it down over the Shire Treasurer's head. He thrashed at the drapery with wide swings and, in his fright, struck a fist against the glass-framed picture of the Queen. It crashed to the floor in splinters, dragging down with it the hapless accountant, who really only did Shire balance books on the side.

Wild noises flew around the room. Countless hands fanned at the air, which was thick with heat and fury. Dianne ducked away from the wall of pointed fingers jabbing at her and disappeared into the thickness of bodies.

The Shire President called out for order, but his words fell noiselessly among the swelling din. He stood there like a startled goldfish mouthing mute surprise. He slammed down his gavel time and again until it split in half and sailed off across the room.

In the crush, someone knocked against the heavy, carved, wooden honour board, and the list of fallen comrades lurched sideways, swung back and jumped from the wall. Chairs overturned and rattled across the room.

'Revolution!' screamed Nigs, galloping into the mass with a white-faced Vivian bouncing on his shoulders and grabbing at his ears. 'Revolution for the masses!' he bellowed, thrusting clenched fists into the air.

Dianne surfaced to grab Vivian. Seconds later Nigs tried to head-butt the Shire Engineer, who squeaked and hid under the bench.

'Killer instincts!' screamed Tam, launching himself with a lop-sided jeté into the room. 'Anarchy!' he yelled, grabbing the fat leather-bound minute book and hurling it spinning like a discus at the wall. It hit with a hard, sharp sound, then softly exploded into a shower of loose pages that snowed down over the crowds. 'Crocodiles! Pythons! Alligators, the lot of you! Harpies! Morons!'

'Reactionaries!' Nigs jumped on to the Council bench, looking muscular and massive as granite. 'It's time!' he screamed. 'It's time! It's about bloody time!'

When terror struck it was cold and hard, for it had been a hot and long summer. The call of the siren rang out the wail of danger not unlike the air raid of police sirens – or the fire siren that it was. Silence dropped heavily on the crowd. Tam and Nigs stopped, transfixed by the noise, and with that and with them the Revolution withered.

There was shifting and movement. The crowd suddenly seethed and the hall quickly emptied of men – each one of them Fire Brigade members and all rushing for the door. They poured out of the building and on to the street, running towards the fire station like the flow of liquid. Those arriving first muscled open the big doors to the garage, and the sound of the engine gunning up could be heard from the hall. The vehicle rolled out of the garage – bright red and freshly polished – and waited a short while for the men to clamber up on to it. Then the siren started again, the deep sound of the engine jumped into life and it raced off up the street.

The rest of the crowd emptied from out of the hall. Women ran to the roadside and watched as the engine tore past in a fury of noise and action. Some of the men were pulling on their thick blue woollen coats, others had grabbed their helmets and boots which they donned as they clung to the side railings of the truck. Two youths on the back gripped with both hands to the butt end of the pump, grim-faced and probably frightened as all hell of losing their hold.

The truck passed, and then a stream of cars, as men unable to fit on the truck drove in convoy behind it.

'Christ,' Nigs muttered.

'Jesus Christ,' said Tam.

'And for Christ's sakes get in your car and join them,' said Dianne, who had planted herself beside us. They swung on her. She glared back. 'Go on. Go, you bastards. Do it. Bugger the bloody revolution.' We piled into my car and took off.

It was at the Wirralla turn-off that we caught up with the back of the convoy. The car swooped around the corner, kicking up a flurry of gravel and sliding sideways in the momentum. Tam let out a whoop.

'Plug it,' I ordered, and he did.

Far off we caught the first sight of it, and it stilled the hearts of all of us. I had never in my life bargained for this. A swirling, tumbling cloud of soft grey smoke held a line parallel with that of the horizon. The whole of the horizon. Pushed on hard by the backing wind, it advanced with a speed that made me slacken my foot on the accelerator.

'Fuck me,' Tam muttered, very low.

There came the cars speeding past us full of furniture, children and women. Their headlights were on because the smoke back there must have been thick. Old Mrs Griggs was at the wheel of one, the offspring of the family and much of their clothing piled haphazardly into the car with her. Grim-faced, she tore past and did not see us. The plastic fittings on the sides of the car had wrinkled and shrunk in the heat.

'Oh my holy shit,' said Tam.

'The house?' I said.

'My paintings,' he said.

Ahead of us, the other cars had pulled up by the side of the road. The engine had also stopped, and from it issued all the men aboard. They grabbed knapsacks of water and set off across the paddocks, hurdling the fences and running like maddened ants. They formed a line and marched forwards, looking small and scattered against the wall of smoke. It all looked so pitiful.

'You blokes in the Brigade?' A man's face appeared at the car window.

'No.'

'No matter. Can you handle a knapsack?'

'Probably.'

'Good. Grab one each from the truck and spread out across the front from the others, but stay behind them. Follow what they do.'

The weight of the water strapped to our backs caught us unprepared. Tam, the frailest of us, buckled sideways under it, and even Nigs gave a grunt.

'We go?' said Tam.

We just nodded.

The spray of the water from the pump-action nozzle was fine and frighteningly ineffective. It dampened the grass before me as I advanced with the line of men into the thick pall of smoke. My eyes smarted, and from time to time I stopped to turn away. I pulled the neck of my jumper over the bottom of my face, then stretched it up further over my nose, trying to filter out the smoke as I breathed. It was thick, and hot work, but I knew that removing my clothes would be foolish. It was protection I needed, not comfort.

The fire was now visible, its vivid, angry tongues of orange and red dancing over the top of the grass. It sent up billows of ash and smoke, and the wind whipped it along, carrying the burnt debris high into the air to drop lightly upon us. Crisply, the sound of fierce crackling carried through the air.

'Break!' The call carried far along the line. I turned to see a group of men running away, looking back from time to time to judge the advance of the blaze. A patch of grass near to them had erupted into flame. The ash that now landed about us was not dead. It glowed still red and smouldered in the grasses. Other spot fires were starting around us.

'Break!' The rest of the line was turning to run back to the engine as the front of the fire leaped forwards in patches, joined together and chewed up wide stretches around us.

We arrived back at the engine ragged and panting. Those who had run fastest made it aboard first and lifted the others on to the running boards as the engine started off. We made it to the car and, in the panic of smoke and gravel dust, sped away along the road.

The engine did not stop until we reached the other side of the creek. A man climbed out of the cab and, standing on the step, called out for silence. With only the whine of the radio defying the low roar of the now-distant fire, he called out, 'The fire's spreading east and southwards from Jackson's Corner. We're now fighting the southern flank. We've got to try and stop it from crossing the creek. It'll be knapsacks and hoses from this side of the bank.'

And again we stood facing it, this time waiting for the bright flames to reach us. The hungry line now glowed with shades of blue and purple. It danced and flickered, taunting us all the while from the distance. It spat out wild sparks. It snarled and roared. I looked at Tam. He was drinking in the sight of it, but there was grim fright frozen on his face.

The hoses from the engine played along the length of the opposite bank. They stretched as far as it could reach up one end and down the other, and the men holding the nozzles braced themselves backwards against the pressure of the water, which cut a solid white streak across the smoke.

Embattled and endangered, for I believe we truly were, we watched the spray hit against the yet-unburnt grass, flattening it.

'Remember to watch behind. Watch for the small outbreaks.' The voice close to my ear caught me by surprise, such was my concentration on the scene before me. And then he ran off to tell the next man along.

The mallee gums lining the other bank started sending up a stream of smoke. As I watched, the smoke grew thicker and thicker and then the foliage caught alight. The trees burst open and upwards. Dried leaves and dangling bark flared like torches and the explosion of light lit up the faces of the men. In the stark and shifting flickering their faces glowed red and black and there was a spark to each one of them.

Flares of flame arched outwards into the sky. The ash that landed in the creek died with an angry hiss, the debris swept towards me on eddies of heat and smoke. From out of the heart of the fire came dull moans and sharp cracks like a bullhide whip. I pumped and pumped, flaying the nozzle and forgetting all else.

My water supply was exhausted. My legs bowed under me and, when still at last, my arm hung like a weight, beside me and yet not part of me. Across the creek, the blackened skeletons of the trees smoked and split open, their heartwood scarred and their limbs like a delicate black lacework against the sky. The grass was clotted and charred into a solid black mass that leaked out small feathery lines of smoke. Bent over the solid green square of my knapsack, I watched the guttering flames playing like innocents around the last stands of sedge grass. There was pain in my chest and pain in my eyes and I knew my arms were going to give me all hell tomorrow morning.

I do not remember driving back to the hall. I'm not even sure if I did.

When I arrived, several basins of cold water were standing on the table outside. The other men dashed water on their faces and in their eyes. All of them had skin blackened with smoke, and as I rubbed mine a thick plaster of sweat and smoke came off on my palm.

A woman poured me a cup of fruit juice, and when I finished that she poured me another. The third cup I spilled down the side of my face, for my hands had started shaking. My legs started to give out from under me, and a man put his arm beneath mine and helped me inside the hall. Along the walls were narrow mattresses. He helped me down on one and I saw his red-rimmed eyes and the black rings of smoke-stain around them. He had been wearing glasses. 'It's all right,' he said. 'And I'm gonna grab a snooze too on that mattress over there.' And then a fine blankness smoothed over me.

The smell was acrid and perverse. What should have been the thick and heady scent of summer paddocks was the bitter stink of burn. The sun of the next morning was still red with clouds of airborne smoke. My car they'd found intact and driven back to the hall, so I was determined to set out once I'd downed the breakfast being dished up by the women of the Red Cross auxiliaries. Ample matrons with floral aprons, they served up endless rounds of toast and jam and tea from great steaming urns and cookers that had arrived from God knows where. I could not find the energy in me to say a proper thank you, but I nodded, took my plate and sat at one of the trestle tables to eat.

The faces of the men that faced me were wrung-out and featureless. If they had been friends I doubt I could have recognised them. No words were exchanged.

'Seen Tam?' The voice of Nigs came close, but seemed removed from the rest of his massive body as it folded on to the bench slowly beside me. His face was pasty, his beard matted and his deep-set eyes more withdrawn.

'No.'

'Hell.'

'You – you were the bloke that went cranky.' A man from across the table was pointing at Nigs. 'You're the bloke that pulled the fit in the Council. Went ranting on about some revolution or something.'

Nigs nodded.

'You're him?' the man continued, stopped and thought a while. 'Yeh, well, things happen. Have you had a cup of tea yet? Do you want one?'

It was dangerous, I was told, to drive out that morning. Electricity poles were across the roads and the trees were dropping limbs without warning. Mile after black mile passed the window of the car. The road surface itself was burnt and buckled and once or twice I had to double-back after finding a bridge burnt out. The first time I passed what had been a house I felt a twinge. The brick fireplace stood lonely amongst the rubble. Metal hayshed poles had turned plastic in the fierce heat and bent over double. Knowing what had been and seeing what was left. I rocked backwards and forwards in the driver's seat, chanting silently, 'Knowing what has been. Seeing what is left. Knowing what has been. Seeing what is left.'

There were cattle on the road, for there were no fences left. They were wandering, not knowing where they were going, for they had been blinded and now bellowed in pain. Some had spreading blisters on their undersides; those with open wounds were covered in flies. Some had lost their hoofs and lay in the paddocks on their sides with their legs rigid and splayed out. Soon some man would plant a bullet in the vinegar spot midway between their ears and their eyes, and they would be silent.

My house was not there. The water-tank had collapsed. The chimney was standing. The garage too no longer stood, nor the outbuildings. The row of cypress trees had been burnt black and skeletal on the side that faced the fire. Sitting in what had been the yard was a twisted and blackened mass of metal. There were no windows to it and the tyres had melted into sodden lumps. John Orchard was standing there beside it.

'John,' I started, 'John, have you seen a bloke? A mate of mine . . . ?'

'Tam?'

'Yeh. Where is he?'

'Wirralla.'

'He's all right?'

'He's in the hospital.' He grabbed my sleeve as I turned back to my car. 'You can't see him.'

'Why the hell not?'

'Because you can't see him.'

'What does he look like? Tell me. Tell me, John. What does he look like?' I could feel the strain on the edge of my voice.

'There's really not much to see. There wasn't all that much left.'

'Go on.'

'Just . . . black. That's all. Black.'

'Where was he . . . ? Where did you . . . ?'

He pointed to the rubble. 'There. Inside.'

'When?'

'After. After it had come through. It came up the road from the west. Wind swung around and it circled in from across there. They tried to stop him. He was in a car. Joe Stroud's car. He'd taken it. They told him the road was going up but he wouldn't stop. He yelled something about paintings and swore a lot, they said.'

'And . . . and how?'

'Quickly. Radiant heat. No oxygen. Wouldn't have taken a couple of seconds. Maybe not even one second.'

I found nothing to salvage. The crockery was cracked and no furniture had survived at all. The budgie's cage was twisted and disfigured and empty. Of Tam's paintings and of Tam, I found nothing at all, although I searched until the darkness made that impossible.

We buried Tam at the end of the week. And not the next day, but the day after that, it rained. It did not stop raining for a fortnight. What happened then was the first bright show of new green grass – a fine stubble that spread across the old, flat plains.